SILENT MOUNTAIN GUNS

C.M. CURTIS

kwympublishing.com
info@kwympublishing.com

1st Edition
Cover Design by KWYM Publishing, LLC

ISBN-13: 978-1519525895
ISBN-10: 1519525893

DEDICATION

This book is dedicated to my family.

CONTENTS

ACKNOWLEDGEMENTS

I would like to thank My wife for all her help with this book and all the others. I also want to acknowledge and thank my first readers: Sharon, Morris, Linda, Marni, and David.

CHAPTER 1

The night was bitterly cold. The wind penetrated clothing like ice water. A thin skiff of snow lay on the ground and the wind blew it around like dust. Colin McGrath idly wondered if his fingers had frozen to the reins he held. His horse, as weary as he was, plodded along the familiar trail and picked up the pace when the lights of the town below came into view.

At a particular house the horse turned in and started up the lane before its rider realized what was happening. Pulling gently on the reins McGrath said, "No, old pardner, not anymore. Not ever again. We're not welcome here."

He sat there for a moment, gazing at the house at the end of the lane. Sparks rose out of the chimney, yellow light spilled out through the windows. He imagined the warmth inside. He remembered the people who once had welcomed him whenever he came here and he felt a stab of grief as he thought of one of them in particular who had . . . No, she had never truly loved him; not by his definition of love. If she had she would have stood by him as he would have stood by her, come what may.

Bitterly, Colin McGrath turned back to the road and swung his horse toward town, pushing the old memories out of his mind. He reminded himself why he had come here, why he had made this long, cold ride. He had a purpose in coming to this place, where any man would be justified by the law in killing him; where his enemies walked freely and spent their stolen money. And that purpose was not to torture himself with painful memories.

He had come to kill a man.

McGrath had no illusions about what was to happen tonight. Even if he managed to kill Guy Mustin his chances of living out the night were slim. But he was beyond the point of caring. Everything that had ever mattered to him was gone: the ranch buildings burned, the land and the livestock stolen, his father and older brother—who had built the ranch and who were his only family—killed in the year-long range war. Even the girl who had sworn undying love and fidelity to him had found it too hard to be faithful to a man who was falsely accused and was being hunted and hounded by his enemies.

He had been ready to leave; weary and beaten, and with nothing left to fight for. He had taken a westward trail and stopped at a farmhouse where he smelled the ambrosial aroma of baking bread—something he hadn't tasted in over a year. He liked it hot out of the oven, with butter and honey on it. The memory of it made his mouth water.

A wagon was sitting in the yard and a woman was carrying things from the house and putting them into it. She greeted McGrath with a smile. The smile was forced, but the kindness in the eyes was sincere. She invited him to get down and share her food. The hardships this woman had endured were printed on her countenance, and though McGrath was not good at guessing ages, he knew she must have lived more than sixty hard years. She had been crying, too, he could tell.

He sat out in the yard at a rough-wood table under a tree and ate the food the woman brought him. She seemed preoccupied—she had forgotten to bring him bread. She had wrapped a shawl around her shoulders, and, pulling it closer now, she said absently, "It's coolin' down. Smells like snow."

Chewing, McGrath pointed to some clouds in the east and said, "There it comes."

The woman didn't look. He could tell she hadn't heard him. Something else was on her mind—something huge. She waved her hand at the wagon and said with a quivering voice, "We're leavin'."

"I see that."

Nothing more was said until, just as McGrath was stepping into the saddle, a man rode up on an aged mare, and said to the woman, "Git every bit of that stuff back in the house. It ain't goin' nowhere."

The woman began to wail, "No, Amos. Please. When he comes back, he'll kill you. Please, Amos, I don't want to live without you." She put her face in her hands and sobbed.

"We built this farm from nothin'," said Amos, his voice hard and full of indignation. "Here we raised our family. Here we planned to live out our lives. No one is runnin' me off my own place where I've lived for near forty years! Not Guy Mustin, not nobody else. I'll die first."

His voice softened to something near tenderness and he said, "Now, Louise, you go get your bag ready like I told you. Maybe this gentleman will ride to town with you and see that you get on the train."

By this point, McGrath had pieced the story together. The mention of the name Guy Mustin had given him the final clue. Sitting in the saddle, he looked around the farm and said, "Why would Mustin want your land?"

"Somethin' the matter with our land?" demanded Amos.

Louise burst out, "Amos! Don't start with your pride. Hasn't it cost us enough?"

"Nothin' at all," replied McGrath evenly, "but the man Mustin's working for is gathering grazing land—land that's all in one piece. Your farm is not the kind of land he wants and it's too far away from the main spread he's puttin' together. It would be of no use to him."

"It ain't the land," said Louise, "it's Amos. He reviled Mustin. And now Mustin and his men are going to come back and burn our farm and our house.

"She stood between us," said Amos, in a low, offended tone, and McGrath could see the man's humiliation on his face and hear it in his voice. A woman had protected him. Probably nothing in the world could have wounded his pride more than that. He was a big man, and clearly a strong-willed one, and had likely never backed down from anyone or anything. Now he was willing to risk almost certain death, in order to prove he was not a coward.

Louise spoke again, a sob in her voice, "If Amos is here when Mustin comes, Mustin will kill him. That's what he said. He gave us three days, and that was yesterday."

Mustin would do it too, thought McGrath. The man didn't make idle threats—and he would not come alone.

Amos began removing articles from the wagon and Louise sat on the front steps of her house and leaned forward, holding her apron over her face, sobbing in despair.

McGrath rode away from there, the smell of fresh-baked bread still in his nostrils, and the craving for it still upon him. And so lost were they in their own tragedy, that neither Amos nor his wife paid him any attention. If they had, they would have noticed that he was riding back in the direction from which he had come.

He tied his horse to the hitching rack, walked over, and looked through the glass of the door into the barroom. Mustin was there. McGrath entered the saloon, a slender man in his early twenties, with dark hair and dark eyes and a face browned by the sun, with a wide mouth that had, in happier times, been quick to flash a smile. At two inches shy of six feet he was not as large a man as his father and brother had been, but his life had been one of hard work and survival in a savage country and his muscles were iron-hard and his reflexes snake-quick. More than one larger man had learned that Colin McGrath was not to be underestimated.

It had been a year since his last shave or haircut, a year of riding and fighting, of never camping two nights in a row in the same spot, a futile struggle against impossible odds. A year ago it had been the three McGraths against a numerous enemy. Now he was alone.

The warmth inside the saloon was a welcome thing, and he went over to the glowing stove and warmed his frozen hands. There was not a man in the room who didn't know Colin McGrath's name, but, though they had hunted him for a year, not one of them had seen him close up. None of them now showed any sign of recognition. The locals, those who had known him and been his friends before the range war had changed everything, did not frequent this particular saloon these days. Moreover, Colin McGrath was the last man in the world anyone would expect to come to this town, much less walk into this room and brazenly stand among this crowd of his enemies, warming his hands as though it were the most natural thing in the world.

Presently, when the warmth of the stove had seeped into his tissues and his muscles felt normal and responsive again, he laid the weight of his gaze upon Guy Mustin, who sat at a table playing poker, and spoke the gunman's name in a loud voice.

Sensing danger, Mustin put his hand on his gun, "Somethin' you want?" he demanded. Mustin was a tall man of slender build, well dressed and well groomed—like a gentleman, like a man of means. But his face was not a handsome, or a pleasant one, and looking into his eyes was like gazing into the very pit of Hell. McGrath had his first twinge of doubt as the gunman stared directly at him.

But McGrath knew there could be no turning back now. He replied, "I was just wonderin' if you're man enough to face me by yourself. You seem to be pretty good at killin' men when they're outnumbered ten to one. Kind of makes a man wonder if you've got any real nerve at all."

McGrath saw the color rise to Mustin's face and the gunman stood up. "Who are you?"

"Just a man who wants to see what you're made of."

"Be pretty hard to see anything at all when they carry you out of here feet first."

McGrath said, "Mustin, you are the lowest kind of trash that ever walked on two legs. My name is Colin McGrath."

Mustin's hand was a blur as he pulled his gun.

None of the men observing would have been able to say who was the fastest had it not been for the locations of the bullet wounds on the two men. It was generally agreed, however, that Guy Mustin could be forgiven for the fact that his shot only grazed McGrath's hip, in view of the fact that it can be pretty hard for a man to shoot straight with a bullet hole through his heart.

McGrath re-cocked his pistol, gave the silent room a quick survey and backed out of the saloon. He mounted his horse, surprised to be alive, and rode into the frigid darkness, passing out of the knowledge of anyone who had ever known him.

Later that night, with the bullet graze on his hip burning and throbbing, having consumed a meager meal of tough meat chased by hot water with a few washed-out coffee grounds in it, McGrath huddled in his blanket and thought of warm bread with butter and honey, and it made his stomach growl.

Frank Jackson sat in his private office at the back of his store, mentally reviewing his life. With most of his past life he was not dissatisfied. The present, however, was depressing to him and had been since the death of his wife two years before. And it was this present, which, projected into the future, was making him feel so discouraged at the moment.

Jackson was a wealthy man. He had built his business holdings over thirty years and was proud to be able to say he had done so in a manner of which his father, the most honorable man he had ever known, would approve.

His marriage too had been a good one, and when his sweetheart and wife of forty years had died he had been devastated. They had raised five children and those offspring were a big part of Jackson's current feelings of dissatisfaction. Not that they had turned out bad, that much he could say for them; they were productive citizens, hardworking and responsible. But they were also, in his current estimation, spoiled and selfish.

What did a man work all his life for if not for his family? If not to spend his later years surrounded by his wife and children and grandchildren, loving and being loved by them? He had made sacrifices for his children, sacrifices of which they were completely unaware, and the biggest one had been that of spending thirty years as a storekeeper, locked inside four walls, counting inventory, counting money, doing bookwork; when what he longed for constantly, and at times quite intensely, was the freedom of the open spaces in which he had grown up. He missed the mountains and the prairies, working hard all day with his muscles more than his mind, cooking over a campfire, sleeping in the open, lying in his bedroll at night, gazing up at the vast infinity through clean, clear air. If he had been alone and had not had a wife and children, the life he had chosen would have been that one. But unselfishly he had chosen a different road. And what had it gotten him?

To a certain degree Jackson appreciated the things money could provide, but overall, those things were not the things that mattered most to him, especially not now that Martha was gone. He stood and walked over to a small mirror that hung on the wall of his office and gazed at the face that looked back at him. It was not a young face and when he had been a younger man he would have considered its possessor to be old. But Frank Jackson didn't feel old. He could still outwork a lot of men much younger than himself. He could outride and outshoot them too. But those things didn't much matter in the kind of life he lived.

He was a tall man, well over 6 feet, and he could still wear the U.S. Cavalry uniform he had worn in the Mexican War. True, it was tighter around the waist than it had been in his army days, but aside from that extra amount of stomach fat, which he knew could be worked off with a month of good solid labor, his physique had changed little over the years.

He heard raised voices in the next room and he heard the word 'father' spoken more than once. He realized that they were unaware he was still in his office and were talking about him. It was his lunch time and normally at this hour he walked the short distance to his home to eat his noon meal. His chair was next to the wall and, without any sense of shame, he leaned his ear to the paneling and listened to the conversation taking place between three of his children: his youngest son, and two of his daughters.

The conversation lasted several minutes and when it was over Frank Jackson sat there for a few moments, deeply hurt. Presently he got his hat and left the store, going directly to the office of his attorney and best friend, Ted Brown. They greeted each other and Jackson sat down and said without preamble, "I'm leaving, Ted."

The lawyer nodded, approvingly, "A trip will be good for you, Frank. Where are you going?"

"Not sure yet, but when I figure it out—and that'll be soon—you'll be the first to know."

Ted Brown frowned. "When will you be back?"

"I won't. I don't intend to come back except for an occasional visit."

Brown leaned forward, resting his arms on his desk top. "What's this about, Frank?"

"It's about the fact that I raised a pack of selfish, spoiled kids. They think I'm old and worn out and they want to put me out to pasture. They want everything and they want it now. And as far as I'm concerned they can have it. Why should they have to wait?"

"Now, Frank, maybe you're . . ."

Jackson interrupted him, "No, Ted, I can see their point. My parents and grandparents on both sides all lived into their eighties and nineties. If I follow that pattern I could be alive for another twenty-five or thirty years. That's a long time to wait for an inheritance. I don't want to spend the last third of my life knowing my own children are wishing I'd hurry up and die . . . and, who knows, wondering if at some point they'll run out of patience and slip some kind of powder into my evening milk."

The lawyer leaned back in his chair, smiled, and said, "Now really,

Frank."

"Oh, I know Ted," said Jackson, scowling in slight embarrassment, "none of them would ever do that. That was just a little bit of self-pity, and I'm already ashamed of it." His voice hardened, "But that's the only thing I've said in this conversation that I will retract. Draw up the papers. I want to take some money with me, but it won't be a lot. I intend to buy or start some kind of business, so I will set some aside for that and wire you when I need it. The rest of my money and holdings will be divided evenly among my five spoiled children. If they want to sell everything and split the money, fine. If they want to keep the businesses and manage them, that's fine too. I'm done."

"Frank, you need to think about this. You're angry, I can tell, and I think you're hurt too. But think about it."

"You're my lawyer. Are you going to do what I ask, or will I have to find myself another one?"

Brown was not insulted by the comment. Their friendship was too old and too strong for that. They had spent nearly thirty years, good-naturedly insulting each other at every opportunity. "Do that," he retorted, "and I'll sue you and I'll own your children's inheritance."

"Not a bad idea. Might teach them a lesson. I'm serious, Ted, as serious as I've ever been in my life. I'm leaving tomorrow and you'll be the only one I'll inform as to my whereabouts when I find my new home. Furthermore, you're not to tell a soul where that is. I'll send letters to you to give to my children and grandchildren, and you will remove them from the envelopes and deliver them unaddressed. If any of the ungrateful souls should wish to write to me, they can give you the letter and you will send it to me. Understood?"

Brown's face grew sober. He nodded and said, "Who am I going to play pinochle with?"

Frank smiled sadly. "I'll miss you too old friend, but let's not get soft and silly here." He looked out the window at the distant mountains and pointed to them. "They've been calling to me for a long time, Ted, and I've resisted—because people needed me. Nobody needs me anymore." His voice rose in volume. "But my life is not over. I'm not finished living, and I feel like I have things left to do."

They lapsed into silence for a time, both of them gazing at the far mountains. Presently, Brown said, "I'll draw up the papers.

Tomorrow morning soon enough for you?"

"No, but I guess it'll have to do."

Ruth Moreland gazed down at her sleeping husband and tried to remember what it felt like to love him. She couldn't. It had seemed easy ten months earlier when they had met. But she had been too young, she realized; and she had believed, in the way that young people often do, that nothing bad would come into her life. As she thought about it, she was amazed at how much she had changed and how many things had transpired in those short months.

She climbed down out of the wagon and gazed westward, hoping to catch a glimpse of the wagon train, but she could no longer even see its dust. She had woken her husband earlier when the rest of the wagons were getting ready to depart, but he had told her not to worry and gone back to sleep, saying, "We'll catch up."

Every time he did this he slept later in his alcoholic slumber and each time it was later at night when they caught up with the wagon train. How late, she asked herself now, would it be tonight? How late would she be doing her chores and cooking their dinner? How late would it be when she fell exhausted into bed? And how late would he stay up drinking?

To make things worse, Ruth had taken charge of the child of one of the other women in the wagon train. Mrs. Meier, a German immigrant, who had lost her husband to cholera, had herself been ill and unable to care for Lyssa, her three-year-old daughter, so Ruth had taken responsibility for the little girl.

Angry now, Ruth went back into the wagon, woke the sleeping child with a kiss, and in a loud voice spoke her husband's name, "Carl!"

Roused from his slumber, Carl rolled over, looked at her, and said irritably, "What?"

"We have to go. We have to catch up with the other wagons."

He chuckled and said, "They're going to have to catch up with us."

"What do you mean?"

"You'll see."

Three hours later she did see. In a saloon in the last town they had passed through, Carl had learned of a shortcut. And, secure in his belief that it would work; he had allowed himself to stay up later that night, drink more, and sleep longer. But the shortcut had turned out to be a trail fit only for a stout-hearted traveler on horseback, and Ruth understood why it was not used by the wagon trains.

They had come to a point where there was a steep upward incline next to a ravine that carried a swift-flowing river. Carl sat on the seat of the wagon, whipping and cursing the team mercilessly, while Ruth, with Lyssa following safely on the side of the trail, leaned her shoulder against a rear wheel, doing what she could to help the laboring mules.

The wheel Ruth was pushing crossed a flat rock and tilted the rock's back edge upward. Ruth's foot slipped under the rock just as the wheel rocked backward, putting the weight of the wagon on the rock. She screamed as she felt bones break in her foot.

Hearing his wife scream, Carl reined in the team, wrapped the reins around the brake handle, jumped off the wagon, and ran back.

"No," she screamed at him, "it's on my foot!" She motioned for him to get back on the wagon, but he came back to her.

"What's wrong?"

"It's on my foot, move the wagon!"

He bent down and began trying to lift the rock, but with the weight of the wagon he was unable to make it budge. Crying out in agony, Ruth pushed him away. Tears ran down her face, but she forced calmness into her voice and said, "Go up there and move the wagon."

As he ran forward, she sobbed, "Why can't he ever do anything right?"

She became aware that Lyssa was standing next to her, screaming in fear. Calming herself for the child's sake, Ruth said, "It's all right, honey, it's all right. Go over there and sit down. Everything is fine."

Carl moved the team forward and Ruth freed her foot, hobbled over to where Lyssa stood, and sat on a rock. Watching her husband whip and curse the straining mules forward, she worried about the left trace of the harness. Carl had been promising to fix it for weeks but hadn't gotten around to it. Now, on this dangerous grade, she prayed it would take the strain.

It didn't.

When the trace broke, the left wheel mule suddenly lurched

forward and lost its footing on the slick rock. The right lead mule panicked and jerked to the right and suddenly three of the four mules were down. The wagon began rolling backward, pulling the mules with it. Rapidly it picked up speed, and when one of the front wheels hit a rock, the wagon veered and slid to the edge of the ravine.

One of the fallen mules had managed to regain its feet, and the two standing animals were scrabbling with their hooves, trying to pull the wagon forward. For a moment, Ruth thought it would happen as she rushed toward them on her crippled foot, but the weight of the wagon on the grade was too much and it went over the edge. Carl had apparently been unaware of how close the wagon was to the edge, and when he finally saw, he jumped.

But the wagon was already going over and Carl's leap was too late. The mules were pulled over the top of him as they were dragged into the ravine, and Carl was carried along with them.

Screaming Carl's name, Ruth hobbled as fast as she could to the rim of the ravine. The wagon had overturned in the river and Ruth saw her possessions being carried away by the swift water. She went back for Lyssa and together they made their way down the brushy side of the ravine, sometimes sliding in the loose dirt, the pain in Ruth's foot making the short trip almost unbearable. The mules were dead, two of them lying in the water, the other two on the low river bank. Carl was lying beneath one of these and Ruth quickly ascertained that he was dead too.

She picked up the child and sat on a rock. For a time she remained there, weeping in despair, holding the frightened girl and rocking back and forth until she fell asleep. Ruth placed her in the shade of a small tree and knelt beside her, stroking her head and kissing her small face. Presently, she stood and looked around, taking stock of the situation. There was nothing about it that did not seem hopeless.

She struggled for over an hour to extricate Carl's body from beneath the dead mule, and when it was free, she rested again. Lyssa was awake now, crying from hunger.

Foraging in the trail of debris scattered by the wagon on its way down to the river, Ruth found a few crackers and an apple. After they had eaten part of this meager remnant, she rocked Lyssa and sang to her until the child fell asleep again, and then, at the expense of horrible pain in her broken foot, she dragged Carl's body up the side of the ravine to a narrow shelf above the high water line, and, having no implement for digging, she spent nearly two hours gathering rocks to pile on top of his body. She was angry with Carl for stupidly getting them into this situation and then stupidly getting himself killed, but still she didn't want his mortal remains to be eaten and scattered like common carrion.

Sitting beside the sleeping child, stroking her fine yellow hair, Ruth realized how much she had grown attached to Mrs. Meier's little girl. She worried for the safety of the child, and she worried about Mrs. Meier's concern when she and Carl and the child didn't show up tonight to camp with the rest of the company.

"We should have come by train," she said to herself. She had suggested that to Carl—they had even quarreled about it—but Carl always did what he wanted to do. He had said, "We can take more of our things in a wagon than on a train, and when we get to California we can sell the wagon and mules to help us get our start."

And now the wagon was gone, and their things were gone, and the mules were dead, and Carl . . . was lying under a pile of rocks.

Ruth considered what to do next. She couldn't walk very fast with her broken foot, but neither could she and Lyssa stay in this ravine. It would be full of predators tonight and for many nights to come until the carcasses of the mules were completely consumed and their bones picked clean.

She made an attempt to get out to the wagon, but the swiftness of the water and her broken foot made it impossible. And the last thing she wanted was to get herself drowned and leave Lyssa here alone to be eaten by wolves. She woke the child and said, "Honey, we're going for a walk. Does that sound fun?"

Lyssa nodded. The child was frightened, Ruth could tell. She had no way of understanding the events that had befallen them, and she clung to Ruth, not wanting to let her out of her sight.

Ruth found a long piece of driftwood to use as a crutch, and together she and Lyssa climbed up the side of the ravine and finished the ascent up the steep trail to the top of the hill. The empty landscape stretched out before her, the trail cutting through it for miles, finally to be lost on the far side of a rise. It was rugged country, with sheer-sided bluffs and ravines so steep the blazers of the trail had been forced to circumvent, rather than cross them. The ground supported a goodly variety of brush but few trees, and these were stunted, sometimes twisted by the wind.

She limped along, sometimes carrying the child, but mostly letting her walk. The trail was seldom level. If she was not struggling uphill, she was walking—sometimes almost sliding—downhill. Ruth was no tracker, but it didn't take a tracker to see that this trail was little-used and that it had had no use recently, a fact that made her feel more alone and afraid. She tried not to think about her dead husband because when she did all she felt was anger. She knew there was no hope of catching up with the wagon train, but there had to be a town up ahead somewhere.

In the last town they had passed through, when they were still with the wagon company, they had been informed of some recent Indian attacks in the area and had been urged to be cautious. Now Ruth lived in fear of encountering those Indians.

On the second day she did.

The previous night she had found partial shelter among some boulders on the side of the hill and by adding sticks and brush she had created a wind break; there, she and Lyssa had spent the night. Ruth had gone to bed hungry that night, not wanting to eat any more of the crackers herself. They were the only food left and the child needed nourishment.

When the sun came up, affording her a view of the trail from her high position, she saw it stretch almost in a straight line across desolate and open country, filled with sage brush and rocks and little else. She was nearly overwhelmed by despair.

She shook Lyssa awake and for reasons she did not attempt to understand she moistened part of the hem of her skirt and washed the child's face. Then, using her fingers, she combed the tangled blond hair as best she could.

Picking up her crutch and taking Lyssa by the hand she began to stand up. As she did she became aware of a small group of mounted Indians on the trail below. There were three of them. One was turned facing away from her, scanning the distance. Another was looking down at the trail, no doubt scrutinizing it for tracks of human, animal, or wagon. One of them, however, was looking in her direction. She ducked back into the shelter and peered out. Had he seen her? He continued to gaze in her direction.

This Indian rode up the trail and out of sight behind the hill. Ruth sat in terrified suspense. Some of the others were watching him, but he had not to her knowledge spoken to any of them. She watched and waited. The urge was on her to run, but she understood the foolishness of that. She could not escape these men. Her only chance was to hide.

The Indian made no sound, but suddenly his face appeared before her as he leaned around the boulder, peering into her little shelter. Ruth would have screamed had not shock and fear stolen her voice. The most she saw of the Indian was his head and shoulders and one arm—and the hand that held the tomahawk.

For an agonizing moment she stared at him as he stared back. Lyssa made a small sound and the Indian's eyes flicked to her. She showed no fear; she was too young to understand her peril. She extended a hand that held a cracker. The Indian looked at the cracker and ever after Ruth was convinced that, though there was no change in his expression, there was some softening of his features. And then he was gone.

She waited. What would he do? Would he return? Would he tell his companions? Would they come up? And then what?

After a tense few minutes, she saw the Indian rejoin his companions. She faintly heard the sounds of the few words they exchanged, words she did not understand, but none of them looked in her direction. Finally, leaving the trail, the group rode south, and Ruth sat watching as they slowly disappeared from her view.

Like every white person in the country, Ruth had heard stories of Indian massacres. She knew she was in Indian country now, and she felt the terror of being alone and helpless in these circumstances. And in the days that followed she stayed alert and frequently sought high ground in order to watch her back trail.

On the fourth day after Carl's death, peering over the top of a high bluff, she saw a party of six mounted Indians in the distance. They were clearly following her trail. She involuntarily sucked in her breath as fear washed through her. How could she and Lyssa hope to escape?

She slid down the back side of the bluff to where Lyssa sat waiting for her, pulled the girl to her feet and in a barely controlled voice said, "We're going to have to walk faster now, Honey."

Ruth was not a frontier woman, but she understood that disguising a trail from an Indian was a difficult thing to do. She had read accounts of people who had cleverly survived being captured by Indians, and she tried now to remember some of the tricks they had used.

There was a creek nearby; she and Lyssa had imbibed of its water just a short time before. She descended to it now and stepped into the rushing stream. She knew the Indians could easily track her to the creek and simply split up, one party going downstream and the other upstream. Eventually she would have to leave the water and they would have no difficulty spotting the signs left by her wet shoes and would continue trailing her from there.

But what if she didn't leave the water? What if she followed the creek for miles?

Fortunately the creek bed was composed mostly of sand and rocks, not mud, and, shallow though it was, its current was swift and her shoes left no lingering tracks. She was unable to use her improvised crutch now, but, fearing to lose it she carried it, sometimes allowing Lyssa to hold it.

Because it was summer, the water was not as cold as it would have been just a month earlier and Ruth was certain she would be able to bear being in it for a few hours. When she came to a deeper section of the creek where the current could carry them, she lay on her back in the water holding Lyssa against her and giggled falsely, attempting to convince the child that they were doing this for fun.

She was grateful for the fact that it was a hot day, because when she stood and began walking again, the sunshine warmed and began drying them so that Lyssa did not complain very much of being cold.

The terrain alongside the creek on both sides was extremely rugged—in places, completely impassible. The Indians would have a difficult time following her, unless they abandoned their horses and took to the water as she had done. Would they do that? She wondered.

Ruth passed several places where smaller tributary streams added their water to that of the creek. Each of these she appraised for its potential as an escape route, but she had been in the water for several hours before she finally saw one that might work.

It was smaller than most, and it drained part of a low mesa, flowing, at its terminal point, through a smooth stone channel with high sides, to roll over the rim, creating a small cataract that fell straight down to the creek. Ruth doubted the Indians would suspect that she had been able to climb up to the stream—if indeed she was able to do so—and hoped they would pass by without investigating.

Carrying Lyssa, she made her way over to the little waterfall and said to the child, "Honey, take my stick." She handed her crutch to the child and said, "I'm going to lift you up there. When I do, I want you to get out of the water and wait for me. All right Sweetheart?"

Lyssa attempted a faint nod. Ruth was worried about the child. She no longer cried from hunger; she was becoming lethargic and slow to respond. Ruth herself was suffering from the effects of days without food, but she knew she could last longer without nourishment than Lyssa could.

Carrying the girl on her shoulders, taking care not to step on anything that would show a footprint, Ruth climbed up to a narrow shelf which was washed with water from the slender cataract. The rim of the ledge was now about six-and-a-half feet above her. With water falling on her face, she lifted Lyssa with both arms, barely able to push her over the edge. She waited, listening for sounds of the child clambering out of the stream, but the sounds of the water drowned out any others.

Now, Ruth began her climb up the wet rock face, wedging herself between the wall and a boulder, using the scant purchases they offered for her hands and feet. She had almost reached the top when her hands failed to find a purchase that was not worn smooth by the water, and her injured foot refused to hold her. She slipped off and fell, landing hard on her back on the narrow shelf.

The base of her spine struck a rock, causing a pain so intense that she cried out. She tried to move and found her legs were paralyzed. Silently she cried tears of agony, attempting to make her legs move, praying for some sensation to return to them.

Slowly it did return and the pain was almost more than she could endure. Eventually she managed to force herself to her feet. She could hear Lyssa wailing up above, alone and afraid, and she feared the sound would lead the Indians to them.

She saw a place nearby, which would afford an easier and much safer climb up to where Lyssa was waiting, but she would have to leave the water to use it, leaving clear signs for the Indians to read. That route was out of the question.

She bent her legs alternately, flexing the leg and hip muscles and restoring mobility. She looked up to the rim of the ledge. It overhung the vertical face below it, which meant that if she fell from there, she would fall all the way down to the rocky stream bed. The thought terrified her, but she knew there was no alternative now, so she started up again.

She gained the rim of the ledge, with water pouring on her, barely able to hold her body's weight with her legs. She found a handhold on one side and, with her feet pushing and slipping on the wet rock, she dragged herself up and over, lying face down in the stream, her legs sticking out over the rim.

There was nothing substantial here to grab hold of, and she struggled against the current that threatened to wash her back over the edge. It was all she could do to hold her head above the surface of the water and in this position, with her back arched, her head pulled all the way back, she remained for several minutes, unable to move forward, trying to keep from being swept backward. She was aware that Lyssa was there, and that she had stopped crying. This, at least, was a relief.

Ruth's neck muscles were becoming fatigued and her face was dipping into the water. Soon, she knew, she would either have to let go and fall back over the edge to the waiting rocks below, or drown. She managed to turn her head briefly to look to one side and saw her crutch. It was some distance away, and she knew that if she tried to reach it she would lose her tenuous purchase on the smooth, wet rock. She tried to talk to Lyssa, but the lower half of her face was in the water, making the words unintelligible.

She made a huge effort to lift her head and speak to the child, but Lyssa clearly did not understand her. Her muscles were weakening and she felt as though the current were fighting more strongly against her. Finally she managed to scream, "Stick." And she used her eyes and head to direct Lyssa's attention to the stick.

The girl walked over to the crutch and picked it up. Ruth nodded her head in approval. Lyssa held out the stick and Ruth grabbed it with one hand, simultaneously rolling onto her back. The current took her now and as her lower body slid over the edge, she caught the ends of the stick on the rock on either side of the channel and held on.

Now, most of her body was dangling over the edge, the force of the water dragging at it. She pulled with all her strength, and slowly inched her way up to where she was finally sitting on the rim with her legs dangling, the water rushing around her and pouring out into open air.

Gasping from exertion she pushed against the stick and managed to stand up, spreading her legs so that her feet were on the rims of the channel. The pain in the base of her spine was almost unbearable in this position.

But, now that she was standing, there was no risk of being carried away by the water. She turned around, and, using the narrow pathway of dry rock that Lyssa must have also used, she made her way over to where the child stood watching her. Lyssa was sniffling, but thankfully she was not making any noise.

They followed the stream for hours, walking alongside it so as not to stir up any mud that would be carried downstream to the creek, where the Indians might see it and follow. Finally, when Ruth could walk no farther, they sank down on a narrow, sandy beach beside a small pool and Lyssa immediately fell asleep.

Ruth had not removed the shoe from her broken foot since the day of the injury, fearing it would swell and she would be unable to get the shoe back on. Now, she removed both shoes to allow the sun to dry them and was shocked at the dark blue bruising all around the injured foot. She rubbed it for a few minutes and then, exhausted, lay back and fell asleep next to Lyssa.

They slept there for several hours in the warm sand with the sun drawing the wetness out of their clothes. When Ruth awoke, the sun was lowering in the west and Lyssa was awake. Ruth looked around apprehensively and, satisfied that there were no Indians around, she looked back at Lyssa. The child was sitting next to her and must have been watching her as she slept. Ruth felt a wave of love for this little girl who had borne her trials so well. She smiled at the child and received a wan smile in return.

After a while, Lyssa, hungry and weak, fell asleep again.Ruth sat up and found that her spine and hips and injured foot were stiff and painful when she moved. Stiffly, awkwardly she stood and walked barefoot over to the pool, lowering her hips and legs into the cool, soothing water.

She was still worried that the Indians may find them, but she was not as afraid as she had been for the past few days. She was fairly certain they could never guess that she had been able to climb the wet rock face beside the little waterfall.

Sitting there in the water, she observed that there were minnows darting around in the pool. She removed her blouse and, using it as a net, caught a harvest of the little fish. She woke Lyssa and they sat beside the pool, eating the live minnows. When they were gone Ruth caught some more and they quickly ate them. They kept this up until the pool was depleted of minnows, and then moved on upstream to where there were several other pools, each well supplied with the tiny fish.

Darkness came and they lay on a sandy bank, exhausted again, and, if not with full stomachs, at least with the sharpest edge of their hunger dulled and with something inside them to provide energy for the coming day. Despite her aching bones, Ruth finally fell asleep.

CHAPTER 2

Spring was almost over but the nights were still chilly, and Frank Jackson buttoned up his coat as he sat and drank his morning coffee and ate his breakfast, remarking to himself not for the first time on how good food tasted when it had been cooked over a campfire out in the clean, wild air.

The day after he had met with his lawyer, Ted Brown, and given him instructions on the disposition of his assets to his children, Jackson had gone early to the store and left a note on his desk, informing his children that he was leaving and telling them that he had left information with Brown. Then, carrying his war bag which had sat folded in an attic for over forty years; he boarded a train going west.

He carefully studied the countryside through the train window, paying particular attention to every town the tracks passed through. The scenery gradually changed and finally, mid afternoon on the third day, he knew he was where he wanted to be.

He left the train, carrying his war bag, and walked down the street to a hotel. People he met on the way were friendly and the town wore an atmosphere of prosperity, one of the things that had induced him to stop here. Another was the loading chutes the train had passed as it rolled into town. This was a cattle town.

The desk clerk at the hotel was professional and friendly and he cheerfully answered Jackson's questions. Jackson had more questions, many more, but they could wait. He mounted the stairs and went up to the second floor, then down the hall to his room, where he put his war bag on the bed. There was a pitcher of water, along with a cake of soap and a towel next to the basin on the bureau. He stripped to the waist and washed up and put on a fresh shirt. It was wrinkled from being folded in his war bag, but he didn't care about that.

He left the hotel and walked down the street. He entered a saloon where he bought a beer and began sipping it as he observed the patrons. Most of them were miners, he could tell. He left and walked up the street to another saloon. Looking in, he saw men wearing the garb of cowmen and he went in and ordered another beer. He spoke to a few of the patrons and they were all affable and polite. He told them he was in the market for a cattle ranch and asked if they would spread that word around. They all agreed to do so. He finished his beer and left.

Two doors down from the hotel was a restaurant which, Jackson soon learned, was owned and managed by an attractive older woman named Bonnie. He went there and had a meal and then returned to his room.

He was embarking on a new life and he felt suppressed excitement growing within him. He stretched out on the bed, alternately thinking and reading a book he had brought.

He was awakened early the next morning by a knock on the door. He slid out of bed and pulled on his pants and opened the door. Standing there was a man dressed in range clothes, dusty from having recently been on the trail. He was an older man, with a weather-lined face that wore an unkempt beard and was topped with short-cropped black and gray hair, cut in the way that a man who cares little for his appearance would scissor-cut his own hair. He extended his hand and said, "Harry Gregson."

"Frank Jackson."

Gregson said, "Heard you're lookin' to buy a ranch. I've got one for sale. Double Circle."

Well, thought Jackson, nothing like coming straight to the point. He ushered Gregson into his room and motioned him to a chair. "Tell me about the Double Circle."

"Sixty thousand acres, close to town, plenty of water, good graze, house, bunkhouse, barn, corrals, good pasture near the house."

The conversation went this way; with Jackson asking pertinent questions, Gregson answering with brief, precise information. Gregson volunteered the asking price before Jackson questioned him about it and it sounded reasonable to Jackson. But Jackson was a businessman and he knew better than to walk into any major purchase without researching it from every angle.

"Want to ride out and look at it today?" asked Gregson.

"Got nothing else to do," said Jackson.

"Where's your horse?"

"Don't have one yet, just got in on the train yesterday afternoon."

"You can rent one. I'll go take care of that while you're gettin' dressed."

Gregson was clearly in a hurry to consummate the deal and it made Jackson wonder why. A rushed seller could sometimes mean a better deal for the buyer, but only as long as the reason for the hurry wasn't something that would negatively affect the purchaser afterward.

Jackson got ready, had a quick breakfast at Bonnie's Restaurant, and met Gregson out front. It was nearly eight o'clock in the morning when the two men rode out and nearly eight o'clock that night when Jackson rode back in to town, bone weary and saddle sore, but utterly enchanted by the country he had seen.

There were wide, flat meadows, with ample water and tall grass, valleys cut through by creeks, lined with trees, and always the tall mountains not far away, with stands of pine and aspen. Had he searched for years he could not have found a better spread than the Double Circle.

Only one thing worried him, and that was the fact that Gregson was so eager to sell. Someone in town must have known this. Someone had to have left town soon after hearing the news that there was a stranger wanting to purchase a ranch, and ridden to Gregson's place to give him that news. Nor had Gregson wasted any time in getting into town, finding Jackson, and offering him his ranch.

Jackson debated on whether or not to go to his room and clean up first before going to supper, but his hunger won out and he went as he was, covered with trail dust, smelling of horse and sweat. He chose a table in the corner away from other diners and waited.

Bonnie came to his table and took his order and in a short time brought his meal. Smiling down at him she said, "You've changed some since this morning."

"An inch of dust on a man can do that."

"Hard day?"

"Enjoyable, but long. Getting to know the country."

"So you're planning on staying around?"

"That's my plan."

She smiled as if she approved and went back to the kitchen.

Frank Jackson could not remember the last time he had enjoyed food as much or eaten as much of it as he did that night, and afterward he experienced only a trace of the stomach discomfort that had plagued him over the past few years. On the following morning when he awoke, he realized that it had been years since he had slept so soundly and restfully.

He had hoped the morning would bring him a clearer picture of what to do about the Double Circle ranch. But such was not the case. He still believed the price was good, but he had a disquieting sense that something was amiss.

He rented another horse and purchased supplies for an overnight outing, including a bedroll and some cooking implements—all this with the intention of getting a better feel for the country round about.

He let the horse choose its own gait, while he sat in the saddle, enjoying the scenery and the fresh air and the fact that he had no commitments. He could stay out until he ran out of supplies, or return to town at any time. It was a heady sense of freedom.

Frequently he rode to the tops of hills or left his horse tied below and climbed on foot to get a long-range view. It was beautiful country, and he had never seen finer graze.

From the top of a ridge late in the afternoon he saw something far off that caught his attention. An animal? It was not like any animal he had seen before, nor did it move like a human, unless it was an injured human. He took his field glasses from the saddle bag to have a closer look. After a few seconds he swore softly and spurred his horse down the slope.

The figure in the distance was a woman, and something was indeed wrong with her. As he approached her, Jackson realized that she was carrying a child in her arms, or rather, in one arm. The other arm was occupied with holding the stick she was using as a crutch.

When the woman saw Jackson coming, she stopped walking and sat down on the ground, appearing to be near the point of collapse. Jackson dismounted, took the child, and made a quick inspection of her. She was awake and alert. Her face was streaked with tears, but she seemed to have passed beyond the crying stage. She was definitely weak.

The woman said, "Do you have any water?"

Jackson gave them water and the sandwiches he had brought for lunch, and these they dispatched quickly. There was an acceptable camping spot nearby and he lifted the woman into the saddle, then handed the child up to her and led the horse to the place. There, the woman handed down the child. Jackson set her on the ground, and the woman leaned out and literally fell into his arms. He carried her over and gently placed her at the base of a tree. He brought the child to her and set about making a temporary camp.

The woman and the little girl slept for several hours and when they woke it was dusk. Jackson got a fire going, put together a meal, and fed them again. While they were eating he took a look at the woman's broken foot which was horribly bruised. He bound it up as best he could with what he had available and then told her, "I'll get you to town and the doctor can take a look at it."

She smiled. "Thank you. By the way, my name is Ruth Moreland. This is Lyssa."

"Frank Jackson at your service, Ma'am."

Lyssa had finished eating and had fallen asleep again, but Ruth was taking her time, enjoying her first hot meal in days and savoring the sense of security she felt with this man. He had told her there was a town nearby and he would take them there. She had asked him if there had been any reports of Indians in the area and he had told her there had not been. She still worried about that, but at least now she was not alone.

Looking ahead, she thought fearfully of her future. What would become of her? She was a woman without a husband. How would she get along? She had no money, no home, no possessions, not even any clothes other than the tattered, soiled ones she was wearing, which, even after they were washed, would not be fit to wear in public. She was young and had never been on her own, and now she had a child to take care of as well—at least until she was able to get Lyssa back to her mother.

Frank Jackson would take them to town, but after that he would have no further obligation to them. And in that town Ruth would have no family or friends, or even acquaintances. She and Lyssa would be alone. At this moment, the world seemed a frightening place.

She knew that Frank Jackson was waiting for her to tell him her story but was too polite to ask. Finally she put down her plate and gave him a sketchy narration of events since that last morning when she had stood watching the wagon company depart, while Carl lay in the wagon in his alcoholic slumber.

Jackson nodded frequently, making no comments. When she was finished he said, "You can sleep here by the fire tonight. I'll sit on that little knoll over there and keep watch."

"This is unfair," she said, "We've taken your blanket. How will you sleep?"

"When a man's on guard duty, he isn't supposed to sleep," Jackson said, smiling.

"You're very kind, Mr. Jackson. Thank you for everything."

He awoke to the sound of wood being broken and the smell of wood smoke and realized he had dozed off just before daybreak. Ruth was building up the fire and starting breakfast. Jackson stood up and limbered his stiff muscles. Carrying his rifle, he walked down to the campsite and said, "I thought you were going to stay off that foot."

"I wanted to make some breakfast before you woke up."

"I fell asleep on guard duty. In the army a man gets court martialed for that."

"Lyssa and I are a little more forgiving than the army."

As if having heard her name, Lyssa awoke and immediately went to Ruth, clinging to her skirts, eyeing Jackson shyly.

Wishing he had a little candy to give her, Jackson crouched down in front of her and said, "Are you hungry?"

She nodded.

"After breakfast do you want to go for another ride on the horsey?"

Again she nodded.

"Well then we'll do that," he promised.

On the ride to town Ruth sat behind the saddle and Jackson held Lyssa in front of him, speaking to her often, pointing out a bird or a small animal. The rented horse had a choppy gate and to keep from falling off Ruth encircled Jackson's waist with her arms. She was still exhausted from her long walk and sometimes she leaned up against him, resting her head on his broad back. In this position, she talked to him.

Jackson had never been one to talk much about himself, but for some reason it felt good now to answer her questions and tell her about his life and ask her about hers, hearing her soft feminine voice behind him.

They stopped for a rest and he noticed, not for the first time, that Ruth was constantly looking behind them. Jackson too, as was his custom, often scanned his back trail, but to see her doing it caused him to comment on it.

"There were Indians," she replied soberly. "They were following us."

Jackson could sense the fear she had felt—and clearly still felt. He knew, as did she, what might happen to a woman who was captured by Indians.

They sat in silence for a time, contemplating these things. Presently she said, "How long have you been a widower?"

"Over two years now."

"Carl's been dead a little over a week," She mused. "It seems so much longer."

"It gets easier with time," he said. "You'll always miss him but . . ."

"It's not like that with me," she interrupted. "Carl wasn't the kind of man you miss."

He nodded gravely. "I see."

"I know I should put on a show of grieving, but that would be hypocritical. I'm very sorry he died . . . I didn't want that. And I'm sorry he left me alone, although not because I'll miss him. I know how that must sound, but all I can say is that he wasn't much of a husband."

Jackson nodded, unable to think of anything to say.

She looked him directly in the eyes and said, "There's a time to be sentimental and there's a time to be practical. I believe you need a wife, Mr. Jackson, and I need a husband."

His eyebrows raised a little as he realized what she was saying to him.

She continued, "You have no ties in this place, nor do I. We can go somewhere where no one knows us. No one will know I remarried so shortly after being widowed. What I'm saying is, if you would have me, I would be your wife."

He smiled faintly, looked down at his hands for a moment and then looked back up at her. "Ma'am, a lot of men would think I'm crazy for not jumping at this chance. You're a beautiful woman. But it would be unfair to both of us. I have daughters older than you. In fact, all my daughters are older than you."

"What does that matter?"

"To me, it matters a lot. And what matters even more is that you and I are not in love. You're afraid, Ma'am, afraid of being alone. And you're willing to make a huge sacrifice in order to have security for yourself and your daughter. I don't fault you for that; you have a responsibility to your child. But I was married as a young man, to a woman I truly loved—and she loved me. We shared that love for forty years. It was real. What you and I would have would be pretend. And after having had the real thing, I don't think I could settle for pretending."

Visibly embarrassed Ruth dropped her eyes. "I'm sorry . . ."

"No, please. If nothing else, I'm flattered."

There was a long, uncomfortable silence and finally Ruth said, "I forgot to tell you that Lyssa isn't my daughter. I was taking care of her for a woman, a widow, who was ill. I've got to find a way to get in touch with her so she can come and get her child."

"She looks like she could be your daughter," said Jackson. "Same hair color, same blue eyes."

"The funny thing is her mother has dark hair. People in the wagon company used to tease us about that." She grew serious. "Poor woman. She must be frantic with worry. I haven't been able to get her out of my mind since the day my husband died. I've got to get word to her somehow."

For a few minutes they discussed how this might be accomplished. Jackson knew some people in California who might be able to help. He told her she could even place announcements in newspapers.

Presently, he said, "Well, let's get back on that horse and get you ladies to town."

It had been hours since breakfast and he rode directly to the restaurant. Taking Ruth's hand, he lowered her to the ground, afterward handing Lyssa down.

He swung out of the saddle, tied the horse, and the three of them walked into the restaurant. Seeing them, Bonnie immediately came over. Jackson pulled out a chair for Ruth and she sat in it, holding Lyssa on her lap. Jackson said to Bonnie, "Will you feed these young ladies anything they want?"

"With great pleasure."

Ruth seemed uneasy and started to say something, but Bonnie

stopped her, saying, "It's all right, dear, don't worry about a thing."

Bonnie went into the kitchen and Jackson followed her and briefly told her Ruth's story. He went back to the table and soon Bonnie came out, bringing food for the three of them. She took a seat at the table and said to Ruth, "Do you have any people hereabouts?"

Ruth said, "No, I have no one and nothing. Everything I owned was in the wagon."

"And," said Bonnie, "you can't work with that bad foot."

"I'll work if I have to. I walked on it for a week."

Seeing the steel in the young woman's eyes, Bonnie said, "I should have said that differently. I'm sure you can work, but if you ever want to walk normally again, you shouldn't."

"I'll do whatever I have to. Lyssa and I will get by."

Bonnie patted her on the hand and said, "Honey, you're among friends. You don't have to prove anything to us. You've already proved everything you'll ever need to. The reason I brought it up is because I have a big house and I live there alone. My husband's dead, we had three daughters and they've married and gone, and I don't mind telling you, I'm lonely. It's been a long time since I had company and a lot longer since I had a little girl in the house."

"Thank you," said Ruth, sincerely. "I'll do whatever I can to help out."

Bonnie laughed, "Well, Honey there's nothing to do. All you need to do is rest and let that foot mend. But Lyssa," she reached over and stroked the soft yellow hair, "Maybe she could take in some washing and ironing."

They had a good laugh and it broke the tension.

Bonnie went back into the kitchen while Jackson and Ruth and Lyssa ate their food.

Finished, Jackson leaned back and patted his stomach.

"Do you smoke after your meals?" asked Ruth.

"No," said Jackson.

"My father used to always like to have a cigar after his meals. Sometimes he would let me light it for him." She thought about it and said, "I mean I would hold the match."

Jackson laughed. "For a moment, I had a picture in my head of you as a little girl, puffing on a giant cigar."

She said, "No, they smelled horrible. But I loved my father and thought I was being helpful."

"Is he still alive?"

"Both of my parents are dead. My mother's been dead for years, and Father died just a few weeks before we left to come west. I never would have agreed to make the trip if he were still alive. Like I said, I'm alone."

Ruth and Lyssa finished eating and Jackson carried Ruth over to the doctor's house. The doctor, who seemed to Ruth to be too young for the calling, was nevertheless quite competent. He wrapped the foot and gave her strict instructions to stay off it and see him in a week.

They went back to the restaurant, where Bonnie met them out front. Her house was only a short distance away and the four of them went there together, Bonnie carrying Lyssa and Ruth riding Jackson's horse. The home was a good-sized, two-story structure, with tall trees around it and a yard fenced with the traditional white pickets. Stepping inside, Jackson saw all the signs of a house long lived in, but clean and well cared for.

Bonnie said to Ruth, "You can have the room farthest from mine. That way you'll have plenty of privacy. It's down at the end of the hall, Mr. Jackson."

"Just call me Frank." Jackson took Ruth there and placed her on the bed. Bonnie laid the sleeping Lyssa beside Ruth.

"First thing you'll need," said Bonnie, "is a bath. I'll heat the water. And I'll see what I can hunt up in the way of clothes for you. I don't think there's anything you'll need that can't be found somewhere in this old place. I think I even have some little girl clothes somewhere."

Recognizing this sort of talk as a signal for him to go, whether so intended or not, Jackson took his leave.

Later, clean and with her hair brushed, wearing a nightgown and wrapper that Bonnie had provided, Ruth sat on the bed and sighed. "It feels so good to be clean again."

"Yes, I would imagine so. I don't know when I've ever seen bath water that dirty."

Unwilling to wake Lyssa, recognizing that she needed to sleep, they had not given her a bath yet. Now Bonnie sat on the bed and stroked the child's grimy head. "We'll clean her up when she wakes." Then she said, "You must have had a pretty bad time of it out there."

Ruth nodded. "I've never been so relieved in my life as when I saw Mr. Jackson riding toward us."

"That was lucky," agreed Bonnie.

"Do you know him well?"

"Hardly at all. Why do you ask?"

"No particular reason, he just seems like a good man. So different from my husband."

"He's a man," said Bonnie. "They're all pretty much alike."

Surprised by this statement, Ruth said, "Surely you don't believe that."

"Well, in spite of my age, I can't say I've had a lot of experience with men, but I know what I've seen. And not one of the men I've known could be trusted out of your sight. Maybe your husband was different but . . ."

"No," interrupted Ruth, "he wasn't, but Mr. Jackson is, I promise you."

"You can't know that, dear. Some men are better than others at putting on a good show."

"I can know it," said Ruth. "I offered to marry him."

"Well," said Bonnie, acting slightly embarrassed, "congratulations . . ."

"You don't understand. He turned me down."

Bonnie's eyes widened. "What man in his right mind would turn you down? What did he say?"

As nearly as she could remember them, Ruth recited the words Jackson had spoken. When she was finished they lapsed into silence for a time and then Bonnie smiled and said, "Well you've been widowed, busted your foot, walked who knows how many miles with no food, been chased by Indians, and, as if that weren't enough, you've been turned down in a marriage proposal. I'd say you need some rest."

She pulled the turned-down bedcovers up over Ruth and said, "I've got to get back to the restaurant to help get ready for the supper crowd. Rest as long as you want. I'll bring you something to eat later, and I'll bet we can dig up some clothes for you tomorrow."

It was springtime when Colin McGrath walked out of the mountains and into the first town he came to, having spent the entire winter in the high country. He had spent most of his time alone, trapping for furs and hunting deer for venison, and these things he sold at a nearby trading post where he had traded his horse and saddle for traps and other needed supplies.

Spending so much time alone had helped to foment in McGrath a growing antagonism toward the human race, and it was a sullen and misanthropic young man who walked into town in worn-out boots and ragged clothes, wearing a full beard and long unkempt hair.

During the winter he had been able to save some money, and he planned to spend some of it on a shave, a haircut, a bath, and a new change of clothes, but as he walked past the first saloon on the town's muddy main street, he was arrested by the smell of beer. He turned and stepped inside and said to the bartender, "Beer."

The mirror behind the bar showed McGrath how he looked, and he had a pretty good idea how he must smell, having gone all winter without bathing. He fought back a feeling of self-consciousness, telling himself he cared nothing for people's opinions.

He took his beer to a table, set it and his carbine on its surface, and arranged his position so as to be able to watch the men in the room, as well as those who came in and out. He immediately realized that he was attracting stares, but the air of sullenness he wore and the weapons he carried suppressed any overt ridicule.

Having finished his beer he left the saloon, feeling dissatisfied with himself and angry with the world. It was in this unhappy frame of mind that he walked into the barber shop, sat in the chair, and said, "Shave and a cut," and proceeded to dourly reject the barber's overtures at conversation.

When the barber was finished McGrath paid him and said, "I'll be back later for a bath. Heat the water."

He walked down the street to the mercantile where he purchased new clothing, from hat to boots. These he carried back to the barbershop, where he luxuriated for an hour in the zinc tub in the back room, allowing the hot water to draw the chill of the long winter out of his tissues and bones.

McGrath's supply of money was dwindling fast. He needed a job, and he needed a horse and saddle. The job would have to come first. He tramped back over to the saloon, feeling a bit uncomfortable in his stiff new boots and clothing.

It was a different group of men in the saloon than those who had been there the last time and they paid him little notice. He ordered a beer and took a roast beef sandwich from the free lunch tray at the end of the bar. It tasted uncommonly good. It had been many months since he had eaten bread or beef. Finished, he went back up to the bar and asked the saloonkeeper if he knew of any work.

"What kind you looking for?"

"I'll take what I can get right now, but I prefer ranch work."

"I'll keep my eyes open."

McGrath looked across the room to a table in the far corner where several men sat playing cards. He said, "They look like cowmen."

The saloonkeeper nodded but made no immediate comment. Finally he shrugged and said, "Fella with the gray hat. Name's Decker. Foreman of Spearhead. He'd be the one to talk to."

Turning, McGrath walked over to the table and said, "Mr. Decker, I heard you might be hiring."

Decker was a man in his forties with some graying of the hair that showed beneath his hat. He had wide shoulders, a thick neck, and a chin as square as a brick. He glanced up and McGrath said, "I'm lookin' for work."

"Not hirin'," said Decker, with no attempt at friendliness.

McGrath turned and walked away, giving the merest glance to the saloonkeeper as he walked past. Out on the boardwalk he stopped, thought for a moment, and then turned around and went back into the saloon. To the saloonkeeper he said, "Know anybody else who might be hirin'?"

"Possible. I can ask. 'Case anyone's interested, what's your name and where can you be found?"

"Name's McGrath. For now, I'll be at the hotel."

The saloonkeeper nodded, and McGrath went out again.

The conversation had been overheard. Decker held a brief conference with the men at the table, after which he said to one of them, "Go find out."

As McGrath turned to enter the hotel, he pretended not to notice the man who was following him. While he was signing the register and picking up the key to his room, the man came in and slacked against the door frame, then followed him up the stairs. McGrath waited at the door to his room as the man casually approached. "Want something?"

"Overheard you say your name's McGrath."

"So?"

"You the McGrath that killed Guy Mustin?"

McGrath hesitated and then realized that by this act he had answered the question. "Who wants to know?"

"The man you asked for a job."

"Change his mind?"

Without answering, the man turned and walked away, saying, "Leave the door open."

A few minutes later Decker came in without being invited and sat down. He was accompanied by two other men. He was not a tall man, but was powerfully built. He had a mustache that failed to cover tobacco-stained teeth. His clothes were the clothes of a cowman, and his bearing was that of one who is accustomed to telling other men what to do. He said without preamble, "You're Colin McGrath."

This was a matter that McGrath had worked out in his mind before he ever left the mountains. His first inclination had been to use an assumed name, but something within him had rebelled against that. It seemed cowardly. The gunfight with Guy Mustin had been a fair fight, and Mustin had lost. McGrath did not regret killing the man, and he refused to spend the rest of his life hiding from the fact.

"Uh huh," he answered.

Decker said, "Still lookin' for work?"

"No, I got a job as a candlewick trimmer while I was walkin' from the saloon to the hotel."

Decker colored slightly beneath his tan. It had been a foolish question. "Alright," he said, accepting the rebuke but clearly not liking it.

McGrath said, "What kind of work?" He was under no illusions. When they had thought he was just a ranch hand they had not been interested in him.

"You particular?" asked Decker.

The thought came to McGrath in an instant that it was moments like this that determined the course of a man's future. He had been raised to believe and act in a particular way. But the people who had raised him and taught him that way were dead. And in his mind everyone else, every other member of the human race, fit into one of two groups: either he had known them and they had betrayed him, or he had never known them and didn't want to. Either way, he believed he owed nothing to anyone. And so he answered Decker's question by saying, "No."

Decker held McGrath's gaze for a few moments and said, "We're getting ready to have a range war. We'll need your gun. That's all there is to it."

"Who's going to start this range war?"

"We are," responded Decker. "Matter to you?"

"No."

"Seventy a month. Almost twice what we pay a puncher."

McGrath nodded. "I'll need a horse and a saddle." He understood what Decker would be thinking now. A man could lose his horse. It could die of disease, break a leg and have to be shot, or just get too old for the work. But a good cowman never let go of his saddle.

"What happened?" asked Decker.

"Wintered in the mountains. Found out I couldn't eat it."

Decker stood up. "Lenny, go borrow a horse and saddle from Soto." He fumbled in his pocket and found ten dollars, which he handed to McGrath. "End of the month I'll give you sixty more. Earn it."

Frank Jackson arose early and rode out to Double Circle headquarters. Gregson was in the kitchen eating and he invited Jackson to breakfast. "Already had one breakfast," said Jackson, "but riding whets a man's appetite."

As he ate, Jackson said, "I want you to tell me everything."

"I was plannin' on it," said Gregson, "but I wanted you to see the ranch first, so it would be harder to turn down my offer."

"I've seen it and you're right; it's a nice spread. I'd like to own it. But there's something you're not telling me."

There was a silence while Gregson sipped his coffee, clearly trying to work out how he was going to say what he was about to say. Finally he said, "This spread sits between Treadwell's Spearhead ranch and town. And he wants it, plain and simple."

"Has he told you why?"

"No, but I could think of several reasons. Might be one of them, might be all of them together. Men like Treadwell are never satisfied. Man has one of the biggest ranches in the territory, it worries at him that it ain't the biggest. He looks around at smaller ranches next to him and sees that all he has to do is add them on to his. Now he's the biggest. Makes him feel pretty close to Almighty. Maybe he's tired of havin' to ride across somebody else's land to get to town. Maybe that galls him. Who knows?"

"If you're willing to sell to me," said Jackson, "why haven't you sold to Treadwell?"

"Two reasons: money and principle. Treadwell is only offerin' half what the ranch is worth. He knew I wouldn't take it; he just wanted to be able to say he'd made me an offer. The other reason is, I'd do just about anything to keep him from gettin' his way. He's too used to gettin' everything he wants, either because he has a lot of money or because people are afraid of him. A few years back he hired Ty Decker to be his foreman. Over the past couple of years they've been slowly gettin rid of all their regular riders and hirin' toughs. Any blind man could see what's comin'."

Jackson sipped his coffee, concealing his disappointment. It was just something like this that he had feared.

Gregson continued, "Decker just lately started pushin' on the nesters up at Canyon Mouth. Some of them have already moved out. He'll make a big push pretty quick to run all of them off. Problem is it's not even his land.

"Whose land is it?"

"It's mine, but that don't stop him. I never minded them people stayin' there. They're good people, never caused any trouble. In fact, a few years back we had some trouble with rustlers. Turned out they were hidin' up in the canyon. The nesters were the ones who put us onto them, which was how we put an end to the problem."

"So why don't you fight Treadwell?" asked Jackson and was immediately sorry for the question. But it had been asked and Gregson, feeling its bite, answered.

"Twenty years ago you wouldn't've had to ask me that question. Even ten years ago. I'm no coward, Mr. Jackson. I've fought my battles, plenty of them. I never took a wife, never had a family, but most of these men on Double Circle have been with me for years. I guess you could say we ought to fight Treadwell, and maybe we should. But if we did, inside of a month half these men would be dead, the other half would be hidin' out. He caught and held Jackson's gaze. If it were me alone, I'd still do it. I guess I'd like you to know that about me, Jackson."

Jackson could think of nothing to say, so he merely nodded. He watched Gregson's face as the man seemed to fight an inner struggle.

After a long silence, Gregson said, "You can lie to yourself and not admit it, but when you lie to somebody else you know you're doin' it. So when you talk things out with somebody, you either tell them the truth or you lie. Either way you know what the truth really is. I guess you know what I'm sayin', Jackson."

Jackson nodded. He knew. Double Circle was no longer for sale. He shook hands with Gregson, thanked him for breakfast, and went to his horse. He climbed onto the saddle and sat for a few minutes, having nowhere to go now and no purpose for the rest of the day. Without any real reason for doing so he asked one of the hands for directions to Canyon Mouth and rode off in that direction.

It was a good three-hour ride—mostly uphill—and he watched with great interest as the scenery changed, from grasses and brush to pine trees and aspens, and always, the stately mountains in the background. What he found at Canyon Mouth was a scattering of small farms, widely separated, but connected by a network of rough wagon roads. He knew there would be a sense of community among these people, perhaps even more than in places where neighbors were packed into neat rows, lined up side by side.

A couple of the farms he passed were run down, poorly worked places, but most of them showed the signs of pride and industry. Like any other kind of community there would be many different kinds of people here, but the majority of them would be good people—honest and hardworking.

He stopped his horse and turned around and sat for a time admiring the view which must span, he thought, twenty miles if not more. The horse was tired and Jackson was tired of the saddle. He had brought food with him in the saddlebag, but a hot meal sounded much better so he rode up to the yard of one of the houses, where several children were playing, and sat there until a woman came out onto the porch. She was in her thirties, tall and with a round, pleasant face that reminded him of his oldest daughter. Her hands were wet up to the elbows and she dried them on her apron.

He had his horse turned so she could read the brand if she was so inclined. He wanted to make sure she knew he wasn't from Spearhead. He removed his hat and introduced himself.

A young girl came out of the house to stand beside her mother. She had flour on her hands, and her face shone with perspiration.

The woman said, "I'm Hazel. This is my daughter Abby. Last name is Russell. If you're not from Spearhead you're welcome to get down and join us; we're about to eat."

She turned and looked to the west and pointed. "That's my husband Ab. He'll be here shortly."

Jackson saw a man tramping across a broad pasture, carrying a shovel over his shoulder.

Jackson got down from the horse, and Mrs. Russell said, "There's a washbasin around the side of the house. There's a towel there, too."

Ab Russell was suspicious, and while he washed up he asked Jackson a few questions. Jackson answered them honestly, but he could tell that Russell was not completely mollified. Nevertheless they sat down to eat together. The food was delicious and Jackson told Mrs. Russell it was. The children were mostly silent and Jackson knew this was due to his presence. Having raised a family himself, he had a very good idea how things would have been had he not been there. He tried to make small talk, but nothing of any consequence was said during the meal.   After the meal the younger children went back out to play while Abby and one of her sisters began cleaning up.

Jackson said, "I've been told that Treadwell is trying to push you people off your land."

Ab Russell leaned back in his chair, crossed his arms on his chest, and said, "Why are you here, Mr. Jackson? What is it you want?"

Abby had turned and was watching them. She was a clever girl, thought Jackson, and she was paying attention. He said, "I came out here looking for a ranch to buy. Mr. Gregson offered to sell me his. I looked it over and then he told me the full story and I decided not to buy into a range war."

"Can't say as I blame you," said Russell. He and his wife exchanged a gaze and Jackson observed in their eyes the fear they lived with. And he had a pretty good idea of the sense of injustice that must burn inside them. He would have liked to help them, but he had already fought in one war and he felt he was too old to fight in another.

He thanked them for the meal and left. He looked for Abby before he rode away, but she was nowhere to be seen. As he was riding down the lane toward the main trail, the girl suddenly appeared from behind a tree. She stood in the middle of the trail as a sign for him to stop, and there was no reticence in her demeanor.

"What would you have done?" she asked him.

"What do you mean?"

"Mr. Gregson don't mind if we live here. He and Pa are friends."

Now Jackson understood what she was asking. She repeated it. "What would you have done if you had bought Mr. Gregson's ranch?"

"Abby, I figure this land belongs to you folks. I would have wanted to be friends with your Pa just like Mr. Gregson is."

"Then buy it," she said. "Please."

The depth of the need he saw in her eyes, the pleading, set up a pang of guilt within him. But he was a businessman. He had been a businessman most of his adult life. There were certain rules of business you didn't break if you wanted to be successful. Moreover, who was he to buck Spearhead? How could anyone in these parts take on a ranch that size?

For the second time that day Jackson made his decision, and it was the same one. The girl saw it on his face and she turned and walked away. It bothered him that he felt the need to justify himself to this girl who couldn't be more than thirteen years old. He spurred the horse into a gallop.

He hadn't gone more than fifty yards when he saw the dust. There was a group of riders coming. He watched them for a moment; they were perhaps a quarter mile away. He turned to look at the girl. She was facing his direction. She had seen the dust also. She swung around and broke into a run.

He swung the horse around and kicked it into a gallop. When he caught up with Abby, he reached down and said, "Climb up."

She took his hand and swung up behind him. When they reached the house, she jumped down and ran across the yard, shouting, "They're coming. Spearhead riders are coming."

CHAPTER 3

Ab Russell came out onto the porch, holding a shotgun. His wife gathered the kids and brought them all inside. There were six riders and as they approached, Ab Russell said to Jackson, who was standing beside him, "Lead rider on the right is Ty Decker. The one next to him—young fella—I don't know him."

They stopped in the middle of the yard, scattering chickens and ducks. Decker said, "Mr. Treadwell sends his regards, and you won't need that scatter gun, Mr. Russell."

Ab Russell made no move. He said, "You're on private property. State your business and get off."

Jackson saw a faint play of hardness, mixed with malicious humor cross Decker's features. He spoke again. "Mr. Treadwell told me to tell you he's sorry, but you have one week to get off this land. We're talking to all your neighbors. Mr. Treadwell says that if any of you don't have a wagon, he'll provide one for you. He'll also give each family a little money for seed and such to help them get a new start wherever they decide to settle down. Each family can buy ten dollars' worth of supplies on his account at the store. In order to get the seed money and the store credit you have to sign a paper." He produced a paper and handed it to Ab Russell, who tore it up without reading it and threw the pieces on the ground.

Decker frowned and started to speak, but Jackson interrupted him, "Isn't Mr. Treadwell being a little hasty? It's my understanding this land doesn't belong to him. This is Double Circle land."

"Who are you?" demanded Decker.

"A friend of theirs." Jackson inclined his head toward the Russells.

"Own any land hereabouts?"

"No."

"Then this is none of your business. Gregson will be selling the Double Circle to Mr. Treadwell. They're workin' out the details right now. We work for Spearhead, but we were sent out here by Gregson as part of his bargain with Mr. Treadwell."

"That's a lie," said Jackson.

Decker stiffened. His hand slid to rest on the butt of his pistol. The only weapon Jackson had brought with him was a carbine and it was still in the saddle boot.

Decker said, "You ought to carry a gun if you're going to be talkin' that way old man."

Jackson said nothing and for a moment there was silence. He had been watching the face of the young man at Decker's left. It was a face that possessed none of Ty Decker's hardness or brutality. He wondered about this one. The other four men riding with Decker were not hard to decipher. They were typical hard cases of the kind a man like Decker would hire to do a job like this.

Looking at Ab Russell, Decker spoke again. "Mr. Treadwell is a fair man and he's made you a fair offer. If you don't take it, you'll have to be responsible for what happens."

"And what will that be?" asked Ab Russell.

"This land has got to be cleared. It won't do to have abandoned houses and shacks where the cattle can come in and break through the floorboards and bust their legs. A week from now Mr. McGrath here," with a wave of his hand he indicated the young man, "will be comin' up here with a big crew to burn all these buildings. Ain't that so, McGrath?"

McGrath turned to face Decker for a moment, then turned back and nodded. Decker scowled. "You got anything to say to these folks, Mr. McGrath?"

With obvious reluctance McGrath said, "Be best if you folks did what the man says."

At the beginning of the discussion, Abby had come to stand beside Ab Russell, and for some reason she had held her eyes on McGrath. He had caught her gaze several times during the conversation and she had refused to look away. At first he had thought she was watching him out of curiosity, but now he saw anger on her face. There was another emotion as well, to be read in her expression, and McGrath tried to pretend he didn't know what it was, but he did. It was disgust.

It had been easy to talk about chasing nesters off their land until those nesters had faces; until they became real people who were being subjected to an injustice and who were willing to fight for what

43

they believed was theirs—just as he and his father and brother and had done.

Suddenly everything came into perspective for Colin McGrath. Decker was no different from Guy Mustin and he, Colin McGrath, was no different from one of Mustin's side men. How had he let this happen? How had he allowed himself to become like the people he loathed most in the world?

As they were riding away, Decker turned to him and said, "Didn't exactly earn your pay back there, McGrath. Somethin' eatin' at you?"

McGrath shook his head. Decker opened his mouth to make further comment, but one of the men behind him shouted, "Hey, look, it's Hughey. Ain't that Hughey?"

Hughey, as McGrath soon learned, was a young man whose lower face and neck were badly scarred from what could only have been severe burns at some time in the past. From the cheekbones up, however, there was no scarring and the eyes were clear and intelligent-looking. In them, at this moment, there was no friendliness to be observed. On the contrary, the young man seemed uncomfortable.

"What are you doin' up here, Hughey?" demanded Decker.

"Just came up for a ride."

"Long way from home to be ridin', Hughey."

"None of your business if it is." Hughey fidgeted nervously with the bridle reins.

"Your Pa know you're up here?" said Decker.

"He will after you tell him."

"Maybe I won't. What is it, Hughey? You sweet on one of these nester girls? Cause if you are you'd better ride over and give her a goodbye kiss. Week from now you'll be cryin' in your sleep over your little lost nester girl that had to go away." He grinned, displaying teeth that were irreparably tobacco stained, and the men with him laughed. All except McGrath.

Hughey jerked his eyes up to meet Decker's. "What are you talkin' about?"

"I'm talking about about adios nesters. They're all going to be gone. Your Pa wants them off this land."

"This land isn't even his."

"He's buyin' it, Hughey, he's buyin' Double Circle. You'd best come on home now. You can ride with us."

"I'll ride alone."

"No, it's best if you ride with us." Decker leaned over, grasped Hughey's reins and pulled them from his hands.

Clearly alarmed, Hughey said, "Wait. You're right. I have to say goodbye to someone."

The four riders behind Decker burst into loud guffaws, and a few ribald comments were put forth. Hughey colored, but he pulled his bridle reins away from the grinning Decker and swung his horse away. He spurred up the trail, glancing back apprehensively once or twice as if to make sure he would be allowed to ride away.

After Hughey left, Decker turned to McGrath and said, "Well, you just met the boss's youngest son—such as he is."

Hughey rode up into the trees and waited, invisible to the departing riders. He watched until they disappeared in the distance and then he left the trees, found the main trail, and rode to one of the houses.

A tall, gray-haired woman was working in the garden when Hughey dismounted and tied his horse. She tried to smile at him, but there was worry on her countenance and Hughey said, "My father's men were here, weren't they?"

"Yes."

They stood looking at each other for a few moments; two people caught up in the same tragedy but affected quite differently by it.

Finally the woman said, "Well, what will happen, will happen. Meanwhile, do you want to continue?"

He nodded.

They went into the house and soon the music of a piano emanated from within.

It was late afternoon when Decker and his group of riders arrived back at Spearhead headquarters. Most of the men tramped over to the cook shack for their evening meal, but Decker went straight to the house. McGrath followed him, uninvited.

As they entered the house, Decker turned to McGrath and said,

"Boss invite you in?"

"No." Then he added, "Fire me, I'm quittin' anyway."

Decker's lips curled in a small smile of disdain, but any comment he had planned on making was cut off by Graham Treadwell's brassy voice. "You're what?" He was standing just inside a doorway which communicated with another part of the house.

"I said, 'I quit.'"

"You haven't even got started yet," said Treadwell. "What is it, money?"

"It's alright, Boss," said Decker, "I was going to tell you to fire him anyway."

"What's this about?" demanded Treadwell.

"We went up to Canyon Mouth to call on some nesters and this jasper did everything but invite them over to the house for coffee and cake." Then Decker turned to face McGrath and said, "Mister, I don't like bein' lied to. I don't know if your name is really McGrath or not, but you ain't the McGrath that killed Guy Mustin. I'd bet money on that."

McGrath withdrew from his pocket the advance money Decker had given him in town and set it on a nearby table. "I'll leave tomorrow."

"You'll leave tonight," said Decker, "and you'll leave without the horse and saddle you borrowed, Mr. Gunslinger."

McGrath knew he was being baited. Decker was trying to push him into a gun fight and a gun fight may very well be inevitable. He felt a peculiar sense of calm come over him. His senses were partitioned; part of his consciousness being aware of everything around him and another part being singularly focused on the man in front of him. He faced Decker, his stance and the position of his right hand sending a message.

Decker was no coward, but he was smart enough to be cautious when killing was involved. He was accustomed to having men back down from him, and the fact that this one was not doing so alarmed him. Suddenly, he was no longer so sure of himself. The man before him was clearly willing to take up his challenge. The eyes bored into him, unblinking, and there was no fear to be seen in them.

Treadwell saw this and said, "Not here, Decker, not now. Back away." He said to McGrath, "You sure you want to quit? The job's still yours if you want it."

"I'm sure," said McGrath.

"Your funeral," said Treadwell, and McGrath understood what he meant. Never taking his eyes off Decker he backed toward the door and let himself out. He had purposely left his horse tied in front of the house and now he grasped the reins and sprang into the saddle, spurring around the corner of the house, just as Decker came out the front door.

He heard Decker's deep voice, shouting for men to mount up and he was grateful that there were only a couple of horses still saddled. It would take time for the rest of the crew to be ready to ride. McGrath, meanwhile, would still have to deal with those two or three who would be in close pursuit. They would expect him to ride toward town so he did not ride in that direction. They would expect that if they stopped to listen they would hear his retreating hoof beats, so he slowed the horse to a walk. They would expect to see him sitting high in the saddle so he climbed down.

There was a small stand of trees just behind the house, perhaps a hundred yards from it. He led the horse into those trees and waited. There was a partial moon and he knew it would soon be down. Meanwhile, he doubted his pursuers would think to look for him here. After all, why would a man on horseback remain so close to the place of his enemies?

Over by the bunkhouse there was a good deal of shouting. The hoof beats of two horses could be heard leaving the yard and riding away from the house, then a short time later, the whole crew left. The fact that they had no idea where they were going caused him to smile.

He waited until he could no longer hear their hoof beats and led the horse to the trail. Then he climbed into the saddle and started away at a walk. The moon finally went away and the night became black. He gave the horse its head, trusting its superior senses. He had been riding for over an hour when the horse shied at something ahead. McGrath instinctively dived out of the saddle just as the first shots crashed through the black stillness. He heard the horse grunt and heard it drop. There was shouting all around.

"I think we got him," someone said.

McGrath's gun was in his hand, but he had not fired. Nor did he intend to unless it was absolutely necessary. He had managed to move away from his downed horse. He heard someone in front of him, not more than ten feet away.

"Sing out," the man commanded. McGrath didn't answer.

A gun went off and the bullet passed close to McGrath. The muzzle flame was directly ahead of him. He fired at it and heard the man cry out. Someone else shouted, "Did you get him, Lyle?"

Lyle didn't answer and the voice cursed. McGrath had found Lyle's horse and he leaped into Lyle's saddle. He yelled, "Don't shoot this way."

"Who's that?" a voice called out.

McGrath spurred away, but the ruse had worked. No one dared shoot toward him for fear they may be shooting at one of their own. It only took a few seconds for them to realize what had happened and they began firing blindly in his direction. He spurred the horse hard, knowing that on a black night like this, speed could be dangerous. About a mile down the trail he stopped to listen and heard hoof beats coming on fast. He dismounted and led the horse away from the trail. When the riders had passed, he took a direction that angled away from theirs, leading his horse on foot and stopping frequently to listen.

When he could no longer hear the sounds of the riders, he mounted but continued at a slow pace, trying to make as little noise as possible. He made no effort to hide his trail—that would come later. Right now he simply wanted to get as far away as possible from any place he might be expected to go. And for this reason he rode in a direction that took him farther from town.

In the early morning hours he began slowly angling back around, and daybreak found him on top of a ridge not far from town, where he could see for miles in every direction. He saw smoke rising from the chimneys in town, and at two or three distant points there was the dust of one or more riders, none of them coming toward him.

It was past nine in the morning when he and his tired mount rode to the outskirts of town and McGrath dismounted. He pulled the bridle off the horse and wrapped the reins around the saddle horn, tying them securely. He slapped the animal on the rump and watched as it headed back toward Spearhead. He had no intention of giving Treadwell a valid excuse to accuse him of horse stealing.

He was dead tired, but he was also hungry, and his hunger won out. He walked to the restaurant and went in.

Ruth's foot was healing well and after a few days of resting she was tired of inactivity and insisted on helping Bonnie at the restaurant. She sat a table and peeled potatoes, made pie crusts, and did other things that did not require standing or walking. And when Bonnie's regular helper eloped with a cowboy from a nearby ranch, Ruth insisted on taking her place.

"Nobody will mind if their waitress has a limp," she said, "as long as the food is good."

It was on that morning that Colin McGrath walked into the restaurant and sat down, having been up all night while every man on Spearhead hunted him.

He was in need of a bath and a shave. He had not thought of these things before coming in, his only objective being to fill the great hollow inside him, but when the pretty yellow-haired waitress came over to take his order, he knew exactly what she would think— and she did.

"Looks like you had a wild night," she said with a smile.

"Not the way you're thinkin'."

"Tell me what your stomach can stand and I'll get it for you."

McGrath liked the familiar way she spoke to him, despite the fact that she thought he was coming off an all-night drunk. And he was never sure thereafter if he ordered so much food because he was that hungry or if it was to prove to her that his stomach was sound and his digestion unimpaired.

When she came to take his plates she said, "Keep eating like that and you'll fatten up."

Ordinarily McGrath would not have asked her about her limp, but since she had been so familiar with him he felt confident enough to make mention of it.

"Broke my foot," she said.

"Horse step on it?"

"Wagon ran over it."

He winced in sympathy.

Finished with his breakfast, McGrath left the restaurant and spent the rest of the morning looking for work. He chopped some wood for the barber in exchange for another shave and used the barber's clothes brush to brush off his clothes. He borrowed a cake of soap and went to the creek behind town, stripped to the waist, and washed up.

It was early afternoon when he returned to the restaurant for lunch. Ruth smiled when she saw him and he liked what he saw in her smile.

He found a seat and stared at the menu board on the wall for a time, deciding what to eat. Suddenly he became aware of someone watching him from across the room. He looked over and recognized the older man he had seen the previous day at the Russell farm up at Canyon Mouth. He could tell by the man's face that he recognized him, and there was no friendliness in the eyes. And why should there be? McGrath asked himself. Less than twenty-four hours earlier, he had been one of Spearhead's hired guns.

As he finished his meal he contemplated this latest turn of events in his life. He remembered the peaceful existence he and his father and brother had enjoyed during his youth and he longed for those days. His father had been a man with no enemies. The McGraths were well liked in the area and when they went to town the faces were all friendly. He remembered how people would stop and shake hands and converse. He remembered the respect in their eyes. And then, almost overnight, his father and brother were dead and he, the youngest of the three, was left to fight an impossible battle, alone and friendless.

Later, during his months in the mountains, he had had little human contact, occasionally seeing other people but consistently avoiding interaction with them. Nothing had happened during those months to change his thinking, or to weaken the wall of sullenness and anger he had built between himself and the rest of humanity—until he had met that family at Canyon Mouth: the Russells. The young girl in particular, had impressed him. There was something about her, something indefinable that made him think of himself not so long before. She had sent him a warning with her eyes that he had better not harm her family. The thought of it now almost made him smile.

The woman with the injured foot came out of the kitchen and took a seat across from the older man and they began speaking. They were obviously friends. The man made no effort to hide from McGrath the fact that he was being talked about. He was, no doubt, telling the girl about the incident at Canyon Mouth, cautioning her. And later, when she came and took McGrath's money for the meal, her demeanor was businesslike and cool. There were no more smiles for Colin McGrath.

McGrath knew how fast word traveled in small communities like this. Soon everyone would know about him—or think they did, and he would be a pariah here as he had been in his home town. The taint of his association with Spearhead, with those men who would soon burn farms and homes at Canyon Mouth would cling to him forever like a stench. It was time to move on.

Mentally he counted the money he had left in his pocket. It was enough to buy a worn out saddle and a broken down horse perhaps, but not enough for supplies for the trail. He needed a job. He became truly aware, for the first time in his life, of the value of a man's good name. Because he had lost his good name in this community, he would have to go away. But for the same reason—the loss of his good name—it may be impossible for him to get a job to earn the money necessary to leave. True, he could buy a ticket on a train, but something in him rebelled at the thought of leaving with nothing accomplished. He was a cowman. He wanted at least to leave this place sitting in his own saddle, on the back of a good horse.

He went back to the same saloon where he had met Decker and the Spearhead riders and asked the bartender if he knew of any other ranches that were hiring.

"Heard you'd hired on with Spearhead," said the bartender.

With a dry smile of irony McGrath said, "Hired on one day, hired off the next." He asked for a beer. The bartender drew it and set it on the bar and said, "Treadwell fire you?"

"Quit. Didn't like the work."

There was a glimmer of something in the bartender's eye. He said, "I thought you wanted ranch work."

"It wasn't ranch work I didn't like."

The bartender was pensive for a few moments. "There's a rumor around town about you."

"The one about how I assassinated Abe Lincoln?"

The bartender gave a half smile and said, "Different one."

"What about it?"

The bartender's eyes lowered, "Nothin'. Folks are just wonderin', that's all."

"Let 'em wonder."

McGrath finished his beer and started to pull away from the bar and the bartender said, "There's an old man owns a little rawhide outfit southeast of here called Flying V. Could be he's lookin' for a puncher. He won't pay as much as the bigger outfits, but he ain't a bad sort to work for and he feeds a man good."

"He ever come into town?" asked McGrath, hoping not to have to spend any of his waning resources on a rented horse.

"Sometimes on Saturday nights. Unless you want to hang around 'til then I'll draw you a map to the place."

McGrath considered for a moment and decided he was not in a waiting frame of mind. "Draw away," he said.

The bartender went into the back and a couple of minutes later returned with a sealed envelope and a piece of paper bearing the hastily drawn map. "His name's Vince Hamm. Give him this envelope, would you?"

McGrath thanked him and left. He went to the livery stable and rented a horse, realizing it would be wasted money if this job didn't pan out. The sun was directly overhead when he arrived at Flying V headquarters. No one was around except the cook—an older Mexican woman—and Flying V's Mexican hostler, who, McGrath rightly suspected, was the cook's husband.

McGrath asked the cook where the boss was and she gave a wave of her arm that seemed to encompass the world in general and said, "He gone riding." She smiled and said, "Come. I feed you."

She fed him beans and beef stew and fresh tortillas and kept bringing him more until he finally protested, to her obvious pleasure, that his stomach would burst if he ate another bite.

She led him to the main room of the house and said, "Here you wait."

He sat in an overstuffed leather chair that extruded horse hair from numerous wounds in its cracked hide, and the last thing he remembered before waking up hours later was removing his spurs and propping his boots on the scarred wooden table in front of him.

A man was standing in front of him on the opposite side of the table. He was a small man, lean and wiry and wizened. Wind and sun and heat and cold had had their way with his features during a lifetime spent in those elements. But despite its weathered aspect, the face was not an unpleasant one and the eyes at this moment bore a twinkle of mirth. McGrath was struck by the man's sense of vitality, even standing there immobile.

"I see Maria fed you," the man said.

"How'd you know?"

"Her food has the same effect on me. Makes me want to take a siesta."

McGrath put his feet on the floor and stood up. They shook hands and Vince Hamm said, "What can I do for you, young fella?"

"Heard you might be lookin' for a rider."

Hamm frowned, "Who told you that?"

In answer, McGrath handed him the envelope the saloonkeeper had given him. Hamm immediately opened and read it, the frown lines on his forehead deepening as he did so. He looked up and for a few moments seemed to be unaware of McGrath's presence as he gazed out the window, but finally he folded the letter and stuffed it in his shirt pocket. He said, "Twenty-five and found. You don't need to tell me it ain't enough. I know it. And I know the other outfits pay more. It's all I can pay, take it or leave it." Then he hastily added, "If you take it, I'll expect you to do the work of a forty-dollar hand. If you need to think about that, then go ahead and think."

McGrath didn't need to think about anything; he needed a job. He said, "You just hired a hand."

"Any partic'lar name you like to be called by?"

"McGrath."

"I'm not much on rules, McGrath. I hate people makin' 'em for me and I don't like makin' 'em for other men. Man works for me he knows his job. He either does it, or he's down the road. I've got just one rule: never lie to me. Man works for me, I got to be able to trust him. One lie tells me I can't. Man that'll tell one lie; you never know when he's going to tell another. Lie to me and you'll never work another day for Flyin' V. Understood?"

"That's alright," said McGrath, "but that stick has two ends."

"What's the other end?"

"Don't ask me a lot of questions."

Hamm thought about this for a moment and then nodded. "Reckon that's fair." He extended his hand and McGrath shook it.

After leaving the Russell farm, Frank Jackson cursed himself all the way back to Double Circle for what he was about to do. When he got there, he found Gregson washing up for supper.

"Didn't figure you'd be back," said Gregson.

Jackson made no attempt to disguise the self-reproach in his voice when he said, "I didn't think so either."

"Well," said Gregson, "Wash up and we'll have supper. We'll talk afterward."

The next morning the papers were signed and notarized at the bank, and Jackson knew he had just bought himself a nice little ranch and a packet of trouble.

Out in the street, Gregson asked, "How soon do you want me off?"

"Stay as long as you like. I'll hire you on as a rider if you want."

Gregson smiled. "Thanks, but I'll be movin' into town. All my life, except for the last few years, I was too broke to marry. When I finally did have enough money to support a wife, I was too busy runnin' a ranch to go huntin' for one. Now, of a sudden, I have money and no work to do. I'll move into town, maybe find me a widow lady."

After leaving the bank, Jackson stopped at the saloon and purchased a bottle of the best whiskey the saloonkeeper had, from the man's own private stock. He asked for directions to Spearhead and rode out there. He tied up at the hitching rack in front of the house and was removing the bottle of whiskey from the saddlebag when someone came up behind him and said, "What do you want?"

Jackson turned around and recognized Ty Decker from the previous day at Canyon Mouth. It was clear that Decker recognized him too. Jackson said, "Where's Mr. Treadwell?"

"Asked you what you wanted."

"My business is not with you, Decker. It's with your boss."

"Get back on that horse, or you'll have business with the undertaker."

Holding the whiskey bottle, Jackson turned away and started up the steps. Decker stepped toward him, reached around, and grasped him by the shirt front, turning him around. Without any warning, Jackson swung the whiskey bottle, holding it by the neck, and struck Decker a wicked blow on the side of the head. The foreman dropped in his tracks.

The front door opened and Jackson turned to face whoever was coming out. He had never met Graham Treadwell, but he had no doubt this was the man himself. He was a tall straight-framed man, younger than Jackson by at least fifteen years, with a craggy face and a full head of hair that was just starting to turn gray at the temples.

"What the devil is going on here?" he demanded.

"I came for a neighborly visit and your foreman attacked me."

Two punchers who had been nearby had come over to assist Decker and were now hauling him to his feet. They helped him over to a chair on the porch, where he sat holding his head in his hands.

Treadwell watched him for a moment, then turned back to face Jackson. "What do you mean, neighborly visit?"

"I just bought the Double Circle. Name is Frank Jackson." Jackson extended his hand, but Treadwell ignored it. He was still absorbing the shock of the news that Double Circle had been sold.

Decker was recovering his wits now, and he said, "He was up at Canyon mouth yesterday parleyin' with some of the nesters."

"Why didn't you tell me that last night?" demanded Treadwell.

"I just thought he was one of them. He never told us he'd bought Double Circle."

"I hadn't bought Double Circle yet. I was looking it over. Mr. Treadwell, I came here as a gesture of friendship. If we're going to be neighbors, I thought we ought to get to know each other, maybe talk a few things over. Hopefully we can be friends and avoid any future problems."

He held out the bottle of whisky to Treadwell, who accepted it without comment or smile. "Come in," said Treadwell, and turned and walked into the house.

Jackson followed him inside. Treadwell waved him to a chair but remained standing. He came straight to the point. "You're not from around here so you have no way of knowing how things stand. Yesterday you didn't own Double Circle and now you do. That means you must have bought it this morning. I'll tell you straight: I was negotiating with Gregson to buy the place myself. Now you've cut in on me. It's alright. You didn't know. I'm sure Gregson didn't give you the deal I would have gotten from him, which means I'll have to pay more now in order for you to make some profit. But I'm willing to do that. I'll give you five-thousand dollars more than you paid. We'll ride to town right now, sign the papers, and you'll be five-thousand dollars richer than you were when you woke up this morning. Not a bad day's work."

"I appreciate your generosity," said Jackson, "but I didn't buy Double Circle to turn around and sell it. I bought it because I wanted a ranch. I still do. I looked it over, I liked it, and I bought it. I'm told you have over a quarter-of-a-million acres. That's a sizeable spread. Why does a man need more than that?"

Treadwell spoke and all softness and reasonableness was gone from his voice. "My reasons for wanting Double Circle are my own. I plan to have it, and I'll allow no newcomer to keep it from me. You stepped into the middle of a bear fight. Unless you step out, you'll get yourself clawed pretty badly."

Jackson stood up and said, "Then I guess we have nothing further to talk about." He turned and went out. Treadwell followed him and watched him mount up. He called to one of the men in the yard. The man came over, and Treadwell tossed him the bottle of whiskey and said, "That's for you and the boys." He turned back to Jackson and said, "You should have accepted my offer."

Jackson looked at him and said coldly, "Since we're not going to be friendly neighbors, I'll be blunt. Keep your riders off my land. And that means Canyon Mouth too." He swung the horse around and spurred away.

Treadwell exchanged a look with Decker, who was still sitting on the porch holding his head. Decker stood up, reaching for his gun and Treadwell murmured, "Not here."

When Jackson was gone, Treadwell said, "Decker, come in here," and turned and walked into the house.

Decker was still a little unsteady on his feet so he immediately sought a chair in the front room. Treadwell remained standing. He said, "You haven't made a very good showing the last twelve hours. Last night McGrath backed you down . . ."

"He didn't back me down," interrupted Decker. "You stopped us."

"I stopped you because you were ready to back down. He saw it and I saw it."

"He's a phony," said Decker. "I don't believe he killed Guy Mustin and if he did he just got lucky."

"Nobody gets that lucky."

"Next time I see him his luck will run out."

"How about the old man who just laid you out with a whiskey bottle?"

"I wasn't expecting that. He wasn't even wearing a gun."

"You'd better start expecting things, Decker. That's what I pay you for. By nightfall every man on the ranch will know what happened. I don't know how you expect to boss them after this." He stood looking at his foreman contemplatively. He wasn't pleased with recent events. On the other hand, he understood that Decker's pride was seriously wounded, and this would make him all the more dangerous to the enemies of Spearhead.

Treadwell understood Decker just as Decker understood him. They were both ambitious, but in different ways. And because of this each saw in the other a means to his own ends. Treadwell's ambition was greatness; or that which he perceived as greatness. He wanted to own the largest ranch and be the richest man in the territory. He also had aspirations to high political office and had recently been laying the ground work for that endeavor. He had made several trips to the territorial capital where he had had what he considered to be successful meetings with the governor. He had another aspiration as well, one that he had tried to keep secret: he wanted to establish a town that would grow into a great city one day, a city that would bear his name.

Ty Decker also aspired to power, but it was power of a different kind. While Treadwell was capable of great cruelty in order to achieve his ends, he did not enjoy it as Decker did. As long as he remained firmly placed on Treadwell's coattails, Decker knew he would have the sort of power he craved. And Graham Treadwell knew this about his foreman.

Treadwell said, "Find me someone who can kill McGrath."

"I can kill McGrath."

"Maybe you can, but I'm not willing to risk it. You're the only man working for me who can control this crew of hard cases you've put together. McGrath knows what we're out to do. He can be dangerous to us. He's not afraid of you, we saw that last night. Have someone watch him for a few days. If he leaves the area, then we won't worry about him. But if he stays around, I want him dead. And I don't want him bushwhacked. I want someone who works for me to stand up and face him and kill him. Do you understand?"

"We shouldn't have just let Jackson ride away," complained Decker.

"I don't want any legal trouble right now. Jackson has money—he

57

just bought a ranch. You kill a man like that and people want to know what happened."

Treadwell opened a cigar box that was sitting on a sideboard, took two out, and tossed one to Decker. As he was lighting his own he said, "Politics," as if the word by itself were self-explanatory. He puffed on the cigar for a long moment and said, "I have a political mind, Decker. Everything I do, I do with the political effect in mind. Take this situation with McGrath and Jackson. Two different men, both of them our enemies, but they have to be handled differently. McGrath is a known gunman. We need someone who can stand up to him in front of witnesses and kill him. That makes us look good. We're cleaning up the territory, ridding it of the old, wild element."

He drew a breath of smoke, exhaled it, and said, "On the other hand, if we kill Jackson, unless we're real careful how we go about it, we run the risk of looking bad. There could be an investigation, and we don't want that. But if it looked like one of the other outfits killed him . . ."

Decker was looking at him through unreadable eyes. Treadwell waited for the foreman's acknowledgment and finally received it in the form of a nod.

"What about Vince Hamm?" said Decker. "His spread is so small it don't seem worth worryin' about. Same with Les Perkins."

"Three or four small spreads add up to one sizeable one. As long as we're doing this, let's do it all the way. I've offered to buy both those spreads and they won't sell."

"Perkins would have—you just didn't offer enough."

"I offered as much as I'm going to. There's bad blood between Perkins and Hamm. Make it look like Hamm killed Perkins, have some witnesses to make it stick, Perkins will be dead, and Hamm will hang. While he's in jail waiting for his trial, we can do whatever we want with Flying V. Even if he gets off, there'll be nothing left of his spread by the time he gets out. Do you see what I'm saying? Start this range war, Decker. Get the outfits fighting amongst themselves, and we can blame anything we do on someone else."

"They'll fight us too."

"Of course they will. And we'll win. Your job is to make sure that when it's all over, we look clean and they don't. It's all about politics, Decker."

CHAPTER 4

"Good morning, Tom Lee," said Bonnie to the man who was standing just inside the back door of the restaurant, "We missed you yesterday."

"Yeah," said Tom Lee, "I was . . ."

She cut him off, "It's alright."

Whenever Tom Lee didn't show up, Bonnie knew why. Tom Lee was a drinking man. Ordinarily Bonnie had very little sympathy for men and their vices, but there was something about Tom Lee that evoked compassion in her.

He was a small man, made smaller and frail-looking by sickness and premature aging. He had arrived in town one day from parts unknown and arranged with Bonnie to rent a small shack she owned on the outskirts of town. He did odd jobs for her to pay his rent— which was three dollars a month—and in exchange for food, which he consumed only in small amounts. He did odd jobs for other people in town to make money to buy whiskey, which he consumed in large amounts.

"What do you need done?" he asked now.

"I need some wood split and there's three buckets of slop you can take over to Mrs. Lacey's hogs." Bonnie felt a deep sympathy for the man at this moment, knowing how difficult the work would be in his condition. His eyes were red rimmed and bloodshot, his complexion mottled, and he had lost weight since the last time she'd seen him— and as she looked at him, she realized he didn't have much more weight to spare.

She would not have made him work, but Tom Lee refused to accept handouts, always insisting on earning what he received. And he never drank in public. He bought his whiskey and took it to his shack. He was very unlike some of the other drunks around town who took a handout whenever they could get it and liked to socialize when they were drinking, afterward sleeping it off on the boardwalk or in some alley or in the jail.

Most people left Tom Lee alone, but there were a callous few who would say an unkind word or at times make fun of his last name, which was Maryann. Most people, though, just called him Tom Lee. No one ever referred to him as Mr. Maryann.

The jobs Bonnie gave Tom Lee did not require speed. It made no difference how long it took him to split the wood, and there was no hurry to get the swill to Mrs. Lacey's hogs. So Tom Lee would work a little, sweating profusely, and then he would rest a little. In this manner, he eventually got a job done.

People around town knew better than to ask him questions about his past because he never answered them. He would smile and make a joke, change the subject, or merely turn and walk away. That was Tom Lee.

The woman woke in a sweat. She had had the nightmare again. The worst part was that it was more than a nightmare: it was a remembrance of a real event—an event that tormented her, waking and sleeping.

She lay there for a time, weeping softly and saying her child's name over and over. "I'm sorry, I'm so sorry my precious one."

She was not a person who tried to spare herself pain; in fact, the opposite was true. She relived the whole painful episode in her mind now, torturing herself. Punishing herself. It had been morning. On the previous night, her husband had beaten her again. She had raised her right hand to ward off one of the blows and he had broken a finger on that hand. Her right eye was swollen shut, her face and ribs bruised. The next morning, after frying bacon, she was attempting to pour the hot grease into a can. The cast-iron skillet was heavy and her broken finger failed her. Her right eye was swollen shut and she did not see her five-year-old son standing next to her. But she saw him now in her mind, screaming in pain, writhing on the floor.

She had poured cold water over his burns, then picked him up, and ran to Ana's shack. Ana would know what to do. Ana immediately began applying remedies, working her magic. Then the doctor arrived. He took the boy from her and smeared the burns with butter. She fought to take her child back. The doctor said he would take the child to town, and he told her husband she was hysterical and to keep her away from the boy.

Her husband restrained her and would not release her and when the doctor left he beat her again for harming their child. He locked her in a room and left. Later that day he returned, saying the boy had died.

Eight years had passed. Eight years of anguish. Eight years of imprisonment. When he had brought her the news of the death of her child, her husband had told her how much he loathed her. He had said there must be a special place in the deepest part of hell for a woman who would kill her own child.

And he had been right. She was there.

"This will probably be the last time I'll come up here," Hughey said to Mrs. Smith. He stood up, turned away from the piano, and seated himself in a chair. They sat in glum silence for a time and presently Mrs. Smith said, "I want you to have the piano."

Hughey's mouth fell open. "No," he protested, "It's your piano. I could never take it."

"When I leave here I won't be able to take it with me. I want you to have it."

"No. It's not right."

"You'll take it or it will rot away in the elements, Hugh." She never called him Hughey, always Hugh. "I can't take it with me, and I'm getting too old to play anyway. My fingers don't work like they used to."

Hughey lowered his head and murmured, "I hate my father."

After he left, Mrs. Smith sat, contemplating the tragedy of the boy's life. It grieved her that she could not help him. The boy had talent; he had a great deal of it, and given the opportunity, he could become a brilliant pianist. The two things he would need for that were the two things he would not now have: a teacher and a piano.

She would leave her piano for him. She had already made the arrangements for some men to bring a wagon and haul it to the grove of trees and cover it with a tarp. From there it would be up to Hugh to make the arrangements to have it taken to Spearhead. But she feared his father would not allow him to keep it. And even if he did, who would teach the boy?

She hated the thought of leaving her piano behind, but she was old and the joints of her fingers were stiffening. She wouldn't be able to use it much longer. Her husband had been dead for several years and her children lived in other places. She had made arrangements to go live out the rest of her days with a son and his wife. She would live a thousand miles from here. She knew she would never have a home of her own again, never again have the independence she had enjoyed since she was eighteen years old. But she accepted these things as she had accepted so many others. Deaths and tragedies and losses all had been a part of her life just as had so many things that were good. Every stage had brought different things, good and painful. It was time now for the next stage—the final stage.

She had accepted this, but she worried about the boy. What would become of Hugh? Who would do for him what she had done for him? And she knew very well what that was. Hugh loved learning to play the piano, but the main reason he came up here was for the mothering she gave him. She had recognized this need in him from the beginning and had done all she could to fill it. Who would do that now? Who would take the place of Hugh's mother who had died when he was five years old?

After leaving Mrs. Smith's house, Hughey turned his horse toward the Russell farm. He couldn't stop thinking about the piano. A part of him screamed in protest at the thought of Mrs. Smith having to give away her piano because she was being evicted from her home by his father. But another part of him desperately wanted to own a piano. What would it be like to have a piano of his own in his home; to be able to play it whenever he wanted? That one aspect of the dream was impossible, he knew. His father would never allow it, but maybe he could find a place to hide it and then go to that place and play it every day. And then, as he thought about it, he realized the whole idea was completely impractical, and the realization left him disappointed and depressed.

These were his thoughts as he rode into the yard of the Russell home. Abby was hanging clothes on the line when he rode up. There were a few unmentionables and she quickly gathered them into her arms when she saw him. Embarrassed, Hughey pretended not to notice.

She invited him to get down and he did so and tied up his horse. Mrs. Russell came out onto the porch and said, "Hello, Hughey." She was smiling, but he could see the strain on her face. There was unhappiness behind her smile.

He removed his hat. "Hello, Mrs. Russell."

They invited him in and offered him food, but he had already eaten at Mrs. Smith's house. "I was just riding by and thought I'd stop in for a visit," he said.

"How nice of you, Hughey. I was about to send Abby for some water. Would you mind helping her?"

"Not at all."

They each carried a bucket and they talked as they walked.

Abby said, "Is your father still going to throw us off our land?"

"My father always does what he says he will. Nothing can ever make him change his mind."

For a while they didn't speak, and then Hughey said, "Have your folks made up their minds where they're going to settle?"

She shook her head. "Pa says maybe Oregon."

Hughey stopped walking. "Oregon? That's far."

"I know."

He said, "We would never see each other again."

"No," she admitted, looking down at the ground.

It was as though the enormity of the situation suddenly laid its full weight upon his awareness. He had been dealing with it piecemeal and now, in its entirety, it was more than he could bear. He set the bucket on the ground, fell to his knees, dropped his head, and began to sob.

Abby was at a loss. Touched by his sorrow, she felt tears come into her own eyes. They had been friends for almost two years now—since they were both eleven years old. Hughey had come on an errand for Mrs. Smith, had met the Russells, and been invited back. And since that time he had made it a point to stop in and visit each time he came up.

Hughey had few friends his own age and none of them were girls. He was too shy to talk to girls and was convinced they were repelled by his scarred face. None of the other girls he knew had ever made an effort to get to know him or even talk to him. Abby was the first one who had ever been nice to him, and sometimes they sat alone in the front yard and talked for an hour or longer. He liked the way she treated him. He liked the way he was treated by the whole Russell family.

With the exception of his half-brother, Jake, Hughey felt he had no family. He had no mother, and his father was a martinet who had no time for his boys except to occasionally berate them and humiliate them for something they had done that displeased him. Throughout their lives they had learned to stay out of his way, and when he was in the house they generally left it. From an early age, Jake, the older of the two, had been made to work along with the crew, and now at the age of fifteen he was considered to be one of the hands. Because of this his days began early and ended late and were occupied with ranch work. He had always been kind to Hughey and protective of him, but these days, through no fault of his own, he had little time to give his younger brother.

For some illogical reason, no doubt having to do with his facial scars, Hughey's father seemed to have no interest in him whatsoever and regarded him as being essentially useless. This was both a blessing and a curse. The curse being that Hughey was being taught no useful skills, and the blessing being that, for the most part, his father left him alone. And so, Hughey had complete freedom to come and go as he pleased.

He loved riding up on Silent Mountain and camping out alone, sometimes not returning home for two or three days. Occasionally when he was away on these treks, at night after Jake had gone up to the room the two brothers shared, their father, not having seen Hughey recently, would shout up the stairs, "Is Hughey there?" And Jake, ever loyal, would answer that he was.

Standing above him now, a hand placed sympathetically on his shoulder, Abby still had only a partial understanding of how much Hughey's friendship with her, her family, and Mrs. Smith meant to him. But the deep sense of loss he was experiencing was more than evident.

He pounded the ground with his fist and said, "I wish he would die. I wish my father would die."

"No, Hughey, you can't wish that. Please don't talk that way."

"I hate him, Abby. I would kill him myself if I could."

"Don't talk that way. It's a sin."

"I don't care if it is. And I don't care if I go to Hell. I wish he would die."

"Please, Hughey."

They filled the water buckets and Hughey insisted on carrying them both. Back at the house he would not look Mrs. Russell in the eyes. He merely shook her hand and mumbled a brief goodbye.

Leading his horse, he and Abby walked together without speaking, down to the main trail. When they got there she said, "I'll write to you."

He nodded, finding no comfort in this. Despondently, he looked at the ground and scuffed the dirt at his feet.

Abby said, "Have you ever kissed a girl?"

"Who would want me to kiss them?" His hand came up and touched his scarred face.

She reached over and did the same and said, "It shouldn't matter; not if she really cared about you. Besides, when you're older you can grow a beard and it will cover up . . . you know, all of it."

He didn't like people touching his scars, and he gently removed her hand. There was a quaver in his voice when he said, "Goodbye Abby," and climbed up into the saddle.

He was halfway home before it occurred to him that maybe she had wanted him to kiss her. But something inside him told him that couldn't possibly be true.

The bunkhouse at Flying V was, like the other buildings on the ranch, small and weathered. Hamm had told McGrath that he had only one other rider, a man named Belshazar. He said, "He's a good hand, but he's an odd one. Do your best to get along."

It was just before suppertime when McGrath met Belshazar. The man had ridden in from some distant part of the range, washed up, and gone to the cook shack to eat. McGrath stepped in after him and said, "You must be Belshazar. Do you mind bein' called Bel, or do you want the whole mouthful every time?"

"Bel, Belshazar, say it any way you want. Come tomorrow mornin' it won't matter anyhow."

McGrath didn't understand the comment, but, remembering Hamm's admonition to try to get along, he did not pursue the matter.

Belshazar was a tall man, lean and angular of frame. McGrath estimated his age at somewhere around fifty. He had long hair and a bushy beard, and the dusty, sweat-rimed range clothes he wore had not been near water for a good long time.

Supper was as good as lunch had been and it occurred to McGrath to wonder why the two other men on Flying V carried not an ounce of spare fat on their frames.

The bunkhouse, though small, had been made to house more than two men, and McGrath had his choice of bunks. He decided it would be best to let Belshazar initiate conversation, but Belshazar did not show any inclination to talk, so McGrath found an old magazine lying on the single table in the room, rested on his bunk for a while reading, and then went to sleep. He was awakened early the next morning by the rooster's crow. He rolled out of his bunk at the same time as Belshazar and they dressed in silence.

They went to the cook shack and had a fine breakfast and afterward went out to saddle their horses. Hamm came out and said, "McGrath, you'll go with Uriah today. He'll teach you the ranch and show you what to do."

Confused, McGrath said, "Who's Uriah?"

There was no change of expression on Hamm's face when he pointed to the man who had been introduced to McGrath as Belshazar. Thoroughly mystified, McGrath said, "I thought his name was Belshazar."

"Yesterday it was. Today it's Uriah."

The man McGrath knew as Belshazar shook his head vehemently and said, "Nope, already used that one."

"No we didn't. That was Uzziah."

The ranch hand furrowed his brows for a moment and then nodded. He mounted his horse and rode out of the yard, and Hamm turned to McGrath, grinning. "When he come to work here six years ago, I asked him what name I was to call him by and he said, 'Any name you want.' When a man don't want to give any more information than that I figure there's a reason, so I let it be. He gave me permission to call him whatever I wanted so I've been callin' him by a different name every day. First it was names like George, John, Fred . . . but pretty soon I ran out of common names—just couldn't think of any more—and he seemed to dislike it if I called him the same name twice. It got tougher and tougher 'til one day it come to me that the Bible is full of names. I like the Old Testament ones the best. Every mornin' before breakfast I open it up and pick the name. Only trick is rememberin' it. He never fergits his name for the day and he ain't happy if somebody else does. Keep that in mind. Now you'd better climb up on that nag or Uriah's going to get plumb away from you."

It was typical ranch work. No different from any other McGrath had done and as the saloonkeeper had promised, the work was hard and the pay was poor, but the grub was good.

One morning, when McGrath had been working at Flying V for a little over a week, Hamm announced that he was going to town to buy supplies and would return McGrath's rented horse while he was there. After he left, Jeremiah—that was his name on this day—said to McGrath, "He'll get supplies, sure, but he'll get drunk, too. That's mostly what he goes to town for. He'll spend the night tellin' everybody who'll listen about his son Simon in St. Louis. He's as proud as Herod of that boy, and Simon don't give a spoiled turnip for his old man. Never writes him 'cept to ask for money, never visits 'cept once when he was on his way to somewhere else. The boss is a smart man, only he's sure blind when it comes to that boy. Anyhow, either he'll come home tonight in the wagon or he'll spend the night sleepin' it off in the jail."

When Hamm failed to show up that night, McGrath assumed the latter had been the case. But when by noon the following day he still had not arrived, Jeremiah said, "I enjoy stayin' away from towns. Why don't you ride in and check on him?"

McGrath's first stop in town yielded results. At the sheriff's office, which was located inside the courthouse, the deputy in charge said, "Yep, he's here. We got him in a cell back there."

"I'll take him off your hands then," said McGrath.

"No you won't. Sheriff Wardman has him under arrest. He'll be staying right where he is until the trial."

"What trial?"

"His murder trial. 'Pears your boss killed a man."

McGrath pondered this information for a moment and said, "Mind if I talk to him?"

"Leave your gun on the desk."

McGrath unholstered his '44 and set it on the desk. Hamm was sitting on his cot, looking bored. He looked up when McGrath entered and gave a grim smile. "Well, Treadwell has me where he wants me now."

"What happened, Boss?"

"He framed me up real good. I left the wagon out behind the saloon where I always go. I was in the saloon for two, three hours, and when I come back out the horse you rented was gone. I figured Soto from the livery had come and got it; after all, it was his horse and saddle. I figured to let you settle up with him next time you come to town.

"Comin' back home it was real dark. Some Spearhead riders come up alongside me, stopped the wagon, and told me if I moved I was a dead man. One of 'em clumb up on the wagon seat and took my pistol. Somebody fired a bullet, then they put my pistol back into the holster. Then somebody started shoutin', 'Why that's Les Perkins. Hamm, you just killed Les Perkins.' I jumped off the wagon and hid in some bushes until they stopped lookin' fer me. Like I said, it was real dark. I tried to make it back to the ranch on foot, but come mornin', Ty Decker and some other Spearhead riders caught me. They brought me right into town and turned me over to the sheriff."

"When's the trial going to be?" asked McGrath.

"They haven't set a date yet. But I'm going to beat this thing, McGrath. I didn't kill nobody, and I'm going to beat it. Meanwhile it's going to be up to you and . . ." he stopped . . . "By the way, what's his name today?"

"We just stuck with yesterday's name."

Hamm nodded, thought for a moment, and said, "That was Jeremiah. Well, it's up to you and Jeremiah to take care of the ranch. McGrath, you're the foreman as of now. Jeremiah has been there longer than you, but he's no good at takin' charge."

McGrath nodded, "Alright, Boss."

"Treadwell has tried to get me to sell Flyin' V to him several times, but I told him to go suck eggs. He wants it, and he likes to get what he wants. I've been expectin' somethin' like this for a while."

For a moment neither of them said anything and then Hamm said, "McGrath, as ranches go, Flyin' V ain't much. It's small, the buildings are run down, I've got two hands, one whose name I don't even know and one who's been with me for a week, but it means a lot to me. Take good care of it."

"I'll do my best, Boss, I promise."

"I think I told you I've got a son who lives in St. Louis."

"You did."

Hamm nodded. There was a little smile on his face when he said, "I'm real proud of him. If he was here I'd sure feel easier about things. You and he could probably whip Spearhead together, just the two of you." He looked down at the floor and said softly, "I sure have missed that boy, 'specially since my wife died. Wish he was here now."

They were silent for a few minutes, and then a smile replaced the grimness on Hamm's face and he said irrelevantly, "I never told Jeremiah that one mornin' when I was fed up with his cussed orneriness, I gave him a woman's name and he didn't even know it." He furrowed his brow. "Now what was that name?" He thought for a moment and suddenly his countenance brightened, "Zipporah. That was it, Zipporah. She was Moses' wife. I think old Jeremiah kind of liked that name." He laughed and said, "Someday I'll tell him." He sobered then, and his expression grew pensive and grave and distant, like that of someone who was seeing the future. "Someday I will," he said in a soft voice.

On the way back to the Flying V, McGrath's thoughts were solemn. A weight had been laid upon his shoulders and he felt it keenly. And though it had not been stated in words during his visit with Hamm, they both knew the job McGrath had accepted would involve far more than merely managing the affairs of the ranch. A range war was starting—the first shots had already been fired. Treadwell had every intention of taking over every ranch in the area, and he had the men and the money to do it.

Hamm loved his ranch and had refused to sell it to Treadwell. It would have been easy enough for Spearhead to simply kill him and take over the ranch, and McGrath wondered why he had chosen this method of eliminating the rancher. He wondered, too, how he and Jeremiah would be able to fight Spearhead with all its riders. He would talk it over with Jeremiah. They would have to come up with some sort of plan.

When he arrived at the ranch, McGrath found Jeremiah's horse standing in the yard, still saddled, the bridle reins dangling. Jeremiah was nowhere to be found, and neither the cook nor her husband had seen him since breakfast. Leading Jeremiah's horse, McGrath back-trailed the animal and a few miles up the trail he encountered the puncher, footsore and limping.

Jeremiah stepped into the saddle, took a long look around, and said, "Follow me. We've got to stay out of sight." Following a route he claimed only he and Hamm knew about, Jeremiah led the way and they did not speak until they reached the ranch, whereupon Jeremiah immediately went into the bunkhouse and began stuffing his possessions into his war bag.

McGrath sat on the bunk opposite him and said, "You going to write to us so the boss will know where to send your pay?"

Jeremiah looked at him as though this had not occurred to him. "He can give it to me right now. Where is he?"

McGrath told him about Hamm's situation and Jeremiah said, "Well then, if he left you in charge, you can give me my pay."

Hamm had told McGrath as much as he could about running the affairs of the ranch, including a hiding place in his office where he kept some cash. McGrath found the money and with it he paid Jeremiah, who said, "Listen, McGrath. Somebody took a shot at me out there and whoever it was, wasn't tryin' to scare me. I heard that bullet go right in front of my face. I clumb off that pony like Jehoshaphat. I've never been a man to run from a fight, but a fight that can't be won don't excite me the tiniest bit."

After tying his war bag on behind his saddle, Jeremiah climbed up on his horse and said, "If you have any sense, you'll ride along with me, McGrath; there's nothin' here for you. You know as well as I do they'll hang the boss. Spearhead will be movin' on Flyin' V any time, maybe even today. This war's already lost. We'll go someplace where nobody's heard of either of us. Someplace where a man can make more than twenty-five a month and not get shot at."

McGrath said, "So long, whatever your name is," and turned and walked to the house.

As his next item of business, and with great regret, He dismissed the cook and her husband, giving them some money to live on until things settled down. It would be dangerous for them to remain on the ranch. While he doubted anyone would shoot either of them intentionally, this was war and McGrath knew well that sometimes in a war innocent people became victims.

While looking for Hamm's hidden stash he had seen the note the bartender had written to Hamm on the day McGrath had first come to the Flying V. It was lying open, faceup on the desk, and his written name had caught his eye. Now he went back in and read the note.

Vince,
You know a range war is coming. You will not be able to fight Treadwell without help. This young fellow is the man that killed Guy Mustin. He needs a job. Maybe he can help you. I think he is all right. You are an old skinflint and won't want to hire another hand. But you will not make it if you do not.
Billings

McGrath put the note down, a feeling of gloom coming over him. Once again he had been hired for his gun and this time he had not even been aware of it. He set the note back on the desk and then picked it up again. He went into the kitchen and put the note in the stove. He wanted no one else to know why he had been hired on at the Flying V.

Ruth's foot was healing well, and she liked working at the restaurant. During her working hours, she left Lyssa with a girl in town, who enjoyed taking care of her, and whose family needed the money Ruth paid her. Ruth had written several letters to people Bonnie and Jackson knew in California and in towns along the way, hoping someone could get word to Mrs. Meier, telling her where Lyssa was and that she was all right.

Ruth knew the day would soon come when she would have to turn Lyssa over to her mother and she dreaded that day. She had often wished she hadn't allowed herself to become so fond of the child, at the same time realizing it would have been impossible not to.

Frank Jackson was a frequent visitor to the restaurant as well as to Bonnie's house, and often, in the evenings after Ruth had gotten Lyssa to bed, she and Bonnie and Jackson would sit and play cards and converse. Sometimes Jackson would play the guitar and they would sing songs together, Bonnie and Jackson harmonizing beautifully. Occasionally the thought occurred to Ruth that the two of them looked right together and it seemed to her they would be good for each other.

It would never happen though, she told herself. Jackson was a widower who still loved his wife and apparently had no interest in taking another, and Bonnie believed that all men were alike and none of them could be trusted. Too bad, thought Ruth; they would have made a good couple. On the other hand, there was nothing wrong with just being friends.

Somehow these thoughts made her feel lonely.

The people who came into the restaurant were, almost without exception, pleasant and friendly and Ruth quickly learned that working there was a good way to get to know people in the community and make new friends. She had liked the quiet young man; the one named Colin McGrath, and had been saddened to learn from Frank Jackson that he was a gunman, hired by Graham Treadwell to run farmers off their land. This surprised her. He had not seemed like that kind of man.

When Jeremiah left the Flying V he took a little-used trail he knew of, thinking it would be safe. As he passed between two narrow shoulders of rock he heard a voice off to one side say, "Howdy." And then a man walked out into the middle of the trail, holding a rifle. There were three of them, and one of them was Ty Decker. He went around to the rear of Jeremiah's horse and patted the war bag tied there. He came back around and took hold of Jeremiah's bridle reins. "Leavin?" he asked.

"Uh huh."

"What for?"

"That's my business."

"Hamm's through here. So's McGrath. You're on Spearhead range now."

"I'm riding off it, ain't I? Did you think I could fly?"

"How do I know you're leavin' for good?"

Jeremiah had his pride, but he was not a foolish man and he wanted to survive this encounter. He said, "We don't need to argue about this, Decker. I could just ride away, and you'd never see me again."

"That'd be good," said Decker.

Jeremiah started to rein the horse around, but Decker did not release the bridle reins. He said, "Before you go there's one thing you got to do."

"What's that?"

"Get down from that nag and kneel." At this, there was a general laugh among the Spearhead men. They were enjoying this.

"You can shoot me just as easy up here," said Jeremiah.

"I give you my word," said Decker, "if you get off that horse and get down on your knees, you can ride on out of here and nobody will stop you." He held up his right hand as if swearing an oath. "My word," he said with a wicked grin.

There was nothing on Jeremiah's face to indicate what he was thinking, and a long moment passed. Finally he smiled and said, "I guess not," and went for his gun.

In a small town, supposition becomes gossip, gossip becomes rumor, and rumor becomes accepted truth. What had begun as supposition regarding Colin McGrath had progressed through the stages with a few real facts being thrown into the mix, and the accepted truth now was that he was a hired gunman, that he worked for Graham Treadwell, and that as a part of Treadwell's master plan, McGrath had spread the fabricated story about having had a falling out with Treadwell; a story made up by Treadwell to enable McGrath to get a job working for Vince Hamm.

For corroboration, the proponents of this theory pointed to the fact that a short time after McGrath had started working at Flying V, Vince Hamm had landed in jail, accused of murder, and his hired hand, whose name no one knew, had been found dead, leaving Hamm's ranch in the sole care and keeping of Colin McGrath.

While discussing this situation one evening over a card game, Jackson said to Ruth and Bonnie, "Now that Treadwell has got Flying V sewn up he can turn all his attention toward me."

Bonnie said, "Don't go riding anywhere without your crew. It isn't safe."

Ruth shook her head and asked the question that peace-loving people have asked countless times throughout the millennia, "Why can't people just let other people live in peace? Treadwell has plenty of land and plenty of money. Why does he want more?"

Jackson shrugged and said, "This is the way it's always been in cattle country. Out here grazing land is money. The more grazing land you have, the more cattle you can raise and the more money you'll make. It's pretty simple."

"How can Treadwell be stopped?"

"Right now I don't know," said Jackson. "Maybe he can't. But I'm going to try and figure it out."

Frank Jackson was right in believing Treadwell would turn his attentions to Double Circle now that Flying V was in his control. Spearhead riders began pushing small groups of cattle over onto Double Circle land and Jackson and his riders were kept busy chasing them off. He wasn't sure what Treadwell's next move would be, but he knew it was imminent. He and his men would have to be watchful and ready for anything.

CHAPTER 5

On his first day in charge of the Flying V McGrath readied everything for a one-man cattle drive. He took all the horses, except a select few, to a secluded canyon Hamm had told him about. It was a box canyon that had a brush fence at one end so the horses could not escape. There was water there and plenty of graze for the horses. He had hoped it would be large enough for a sizable herd of cattle, but it was not.

He did not return to ranch headquarters, but riding one horse and herding several others he rode to the part of the range where the bulk of Flying V's cattle grazed.

It was just getting dusk when he arrived and he began rounding up as many cattle as he could before daylight was completely gone. He had chosen this time of evening, knowing there would still be sufficient light for him to do what he needed to do, but dark enough that any dust he raised would not be seen.

It took him several hours to gather the herd and by that time it was well past dark. There was enough of a moon for him to see what he was doing and for the cattle to see where they were putting their feet, and he kept them on the move the entire night and all the next day, stopping at nightfall to give himself and his horses a few hours of rest.

He was doing the work of several men, and keeping the herd together was a job that quickly wore a horse out, making it necessary for him to change mounts often so the animals could rest. The problem was there was only one of him.

Not having anyone to drive a chuck wagon or lead pack horses, McGrath had been able to pack a very limited amount of supplies— just what he could cram into his saddlebags. His meals consisted mainly of jerky and coffee.

He knew the cattle were exhausted, but he didn't want them to get too rested. If they were tired they would be more manageable and have less of a tendency to stray. The herd could have moved faster had there been more riders, but as it was, McGrath kept them moving along, allowing them and himself only short rests.

It was late afternoon on the third day when he caught sight of a rider up in the timber. The rider quickly moved back into the trees, obviously not wanting to be seen. McGrath swore under his breath. This was something he had feared. A man alone with a herd would be a huge temptation to rustlers and outlaws and renegade Indians. Whoever it was that had been watching him couldn't be honest, else why had he moved so quickly out of sight?

McGrath knew how to be watchful without seeming to be, and he spent the rest of the day until twilight in a state of heightened awareness. After dark, he let the herd graze, knowing they were too hungry and exhausted to stray very far. They had had their fill of long walks.

He built a decoy fire in a sheltered spot, where its glow would be seen from a distance. He then ate a hasty meal and sought a safer place for himself. He wanted to stay awake, to keep watch, but he was physically exhausted from too many days of hard labor with far too little sleep.

He allowed himself six hours of sleep and then saddled up and rode back to the place where he had left the herd. The herd was gone. Whoever the rustlers were, they had taken everything but the fire, and it had gone out. He built it up again, had a hasty meal of jerky and coffee—both of which were running low—and afterward set out on the trail.

It was not hard to follow the trail of a few hundred hooves, and, not having a herd to slow him down, McGrath was able to move much faster than the rustlers. He knew what he would have to do when he caught up with them—there was no question about that— he just didn't know exactly how to go about it. That would come later when he knew more about them. Right now, he didn't even know how many of them there were.

It was mid-morning when he caught sight of their dust, and around noon when he got his first look at them from a distance. There were four of them. He watched them the rest of the day, and that night he made a cold camp nearby. But he slept all night, and the next morning he felt refreshed. He was out of coffee and his jerky was almost all gone too. Somehow he would need to acquire some victuals soon.

He did not want to get too close to the rustlers and allow them to become aware of his presence. He did not doubt that they expected him to be on their trail and would be watching for him. And they would kill him on sight if he was not careful.

He was not dissatisfied with the direction the rustlers were taking the herd—it was the direction he would have taken if he had still been the direction chooser—so he was content for the time being to follow the herd's trail, keeping its dust in sight and not wearing himself out with hard work and short sleeps as he formerly had. He would wait for his opportunity to present itself.

Patience was his greatest ally. The longer he waited, the more the rustlers would believe they had gotten away with the steal and relax their vigilance. So, he rationed his jerky, washed it down with pure spring water, rested at night, followed at a leisurely pace during the day, and bided his time.

McGrath was a cowman, born and raised on the frontier, and in his mind there was no doubt as to what must be done with the rustlers when he caught up with them. He didn't have to wrestle with his conscience or mentally debate the moral facets of the situation. Rustlers had to die. It was the law of the range. He knew it and they also, without a doubt, had known what they were risking when they made the decision to steal a man's herd. If he was able to take them without gunplay he would hang them. If not, he would shoot them. There were no other options available according to the frontier philosophy he had been raised with. Every night he cleaned his guns with a rag he had torn off the bottom of his shirt. Every morning he checked the mechanisms and the loads. He would need to be ready.

Late afternoon of the fifth day, it started to rain. The rain came down in solid sheets, and he had difficulty seeing more than a few yards ahead of him. Lightning struck a tree less than half a mile away and the deafening thunder set his frightened horse to bucking. McGrath stayed in the saddle, speaking soothingly to the terrified animal until it calmed down.

He knew the rustlers would not be pushing the herd in this storm; they would have their hands full merely keeping the animals from stampeding. He decided it was time to make his play.

He found the herd scattered in a broad meadow. Through the curtain of rain he was able to make out the dim forms of riders frantically trying to keep the frightened animals bunched. He spurred toward the nearest rider, his carbine at the ready. When McGrath was near enough to be noticed, the rustler turned in the saddle and said something that was drowned by a clap of thunder. McGrath was close now, running his horse. The rustler appeared suddenly to realize that this was an enemy and he lurched to one side, clawing his slicker aside to get to his pistol. McGrath's horse hit him, barely slowing, and he slammed the butt of his rifle against the man's head, dropping him on the sodden grass.

He tied his pony to a nearby tree, checked the rustler—who was dead—donned the rustler's slicker and hat and mounted the man's horse, which turned out to be one of the stolen Flying V mounts. He rode casually across the meadow to where one of the other rustlers had dismounted and was checking his horse's left front hoof. McGrath drew near and said over the noise of the storm, "Lame?"

The rustler dropped the hoof, turned, and said, "Looks like . . ." He stopped short when he found McGrath's rifle muzzle in his face.

"Turn around and drop your gun belt," ordered McGrath.

The rustler did as he was told. Now, McGrath was faced with the dilemma of what to do with the man. This was not the time to hang him, and a shot would alert the other two rustlers and possibly stampede the already terrified herd. He thought for a moment and ordered the rustler to remove his boots. Muttering threats, the rustler complied. He was a big man, with huge shoulders, a protruding paunch, and small, mean eyes that glared at McGrath with a murderous hate.

Tying a man's hands with one hand is not an easy thing to do, but McGrath could tell this was a dangerous man and he dared not put his carbine down for even an instant. He did the best job he could with the man's own lariat, figuring it would hold long enough for what he was about to do.

He made the rustler lie on the ground, brought the slack rope down to the rustler's ankles, looped it around and then between them, and climbed back on his horse. Turning in the saddle, he said, "Make a sound and I'll shoot you to shut you up." He hitched the end of the rope around the saddle horn and, having temporarily solved the problem of what to do with his captive, he spurred the horse across the meadow, dragging the rustler through the rain-slick grass.

It was getting dark now and through the rain he was having difficulty seeing the remaining two rustlers. Finally, he caught sight of one of them over to his right and reined around to approach him. As he drew near he saw the fourth rustler approaching from his left side and realized he had gotten himself between the two of them. They were close enough now that, if he tried to veer off, he ran the risk of one or both of them spotting their dragging friend.

McGrath had never been indecisive. He was born to action. He raised the carbine and shot the nearest outlaw out of the saddle, then wheeled the horse to take a bead on the other rustler. But that one was already spurring toward him, firing his pistol and McGrath heard the bullets ripping through the air around him.

The rustler was getting closer and McGrath was still sideways to him. He leaned forward and then sideways, intentionally slipping off his horse, and knelt on the ground in order to make a smaller target and steady himself for his shot. As he did so, a bullet hit the forestock of his carbine, shattering it and ripping a furrow along his forearm.

The rustler was almost on him now, spurring his horse viciously, re-cocking his pistol, aiming it. McGrath threw himself to one side, pulling his own pistol and firing it as soon as it was up. The man slumped, struggled to hang on, and then fell out of the saddle as his horse thundered past.

McGrath lowered his gun and drew a deep breath, thinking the danger was over. But the rustler he had dragged across the meadow had freed his hands and feet and come up behind. Now he dropped the rope over McGrath's head, jerked it back against his throat, and pulled him over backward. McGrath still had his pistol in his hand and as he raised it the rustler saw the danger, let go of the rope, and threw himself forward, putting the weight of his body across McGrath's chest and head, gripping McGrath's gun hand, fighting to take the pistol.

With his free hand McGrath slugged the rustler repeatedly on the side of the head, arching his back and bucking, trying to throw the man off, but the big man had him pinned with his weight and he stubbornly clung to the pistol, slowly prying it from McGrath's grip with his two hands as he bellowed curses and threats.

McGrath felt the gun slipping from his weakening fingers and when he finally let go, the rustler shouted triumphantly, "I've got you now, you . . ."

They were his last words. With his free hand, McGrath had pulled his sheath knife, which he always wore on the left side of his gun belt. It was a long knife and McGrath kept it razor-sharp.

Using the big man's shirt, McGrath wiped the blood from his knife blade, afterward resting for a while, lying on his back in the wet grass, the sheeting rain falling on him, soothing his aching body. Presently he got up and rounded up all the saddled horses, unsaddled them, and left them to graze. He found the rustler's pack mule and led it to a place where there was a meager shelter beneath an overhanging rock on a hillside. There he wrapped his bandana around the bullet wound on his arm, which hurt fiercely, made a fire, and ate some of the food he found in the saddle pack of the mule.

He sat beneath the overhang, leaning back against the dirt of the hillside, experiencing the letdown that always came when the action was over, feeling lonely and depressed. It would pass, he told himself; he had felt it before. But even his logical mind argued that he really was alone in the world, he really did have nothing to hold onto or look forward to, and the world really was a tragic place. It was very late when he finally fell asleep.

It took him most of the next day to round up the scattered livestock, and late that afternoon he found a boxed valley where he corralled them for the night. Early the next morning he was on the trail once more and by late afternoon he came to the place he had been aiming for: a large valley at the base of the mountains where the grass was up to the cattle's knees and there was plenty of water. He had passed through this place on his way out of the mountains where he had spent the winter.

Leaving the weary herd, he rode to a small settlement nearby; a place so small it had only two saloons. Tying his horse in front of one of them he walked in, bought a beer, and said to the bartender, "Any boys around here who need to make a little money?"

"There are a few farms," said the bartender, "Farmers always need their boys to help on the farm, but if you're talkin' about cash money, you'll probably be able to find some takers."

He gave McGrath directions to several farms, and McGrath met with success at the first one. The farmer, a middle-aged man named Dixon, said, "I've got five boys and I need all of 'em helpin' me. But cash money has been a little hard to come by lately." He chewed his bottom lip, "How much you payin'?"

"Twenty-five a month and all he's got to do is watch my herd."

"He'll need a horse," said Dixon.

"There's five or six of 'em up there. He'll have to take his own saddle and bridle, and a rope."

"Sure. We've got those."

"I'll give you two month's pay in advance," said McGrath. "Fifty dollars. I don't know when I'll be back up here." McGrath had a pretty good idea what fifty dollars cash money could mean to this man and his family and it made him wish he could give them more. But twenty-five a month was generous and it was Vince Hamm's money, not his.

Dixon said, "They ain't rustled cows, are they?"

"They've been rustled once, but I got 'em back."

Dixon regretfully shook his head. "Wouldn't want a boy of mine gettin' mixed up in some kind of feud 'twixt you and them rustlers."

"The rustlers are all dead," said McGrath matter-of-factly. "Their feudin' days are done."

Dixon considered this information for a moment and then nodded his head.

McGrath said, "I work for an outfit called the Flying V. Owned by a man named Vince Hamm. He's the owner of this herd. I'll write his name for you so you won't forget it. There's a chance I won't be comin' back up here, but anyone who comes representing the Flying V will have authorization to take the herd." What he left unsaid was that if no one came within the next two months, it would probably mean the Flying V and its men were dead.

The farmer accepted the money and they shook hands on the deal. McGrath was invited to stay the night and was offered dinner. When he was washing up he took off the rag he had used to bandage his wounded forearm and didn't like what he saw. He asked Dixon if he had any salve and the farmer looked at the wound and called to his wife.

"She shook her head, "Nasty scratch. How'd you . . ."

Dixon cut her off. "Mr. McGrath don't need us askin' a lot of questions, Ma. It ain't polite."

Mrs. Dixon made up a poultice of a particular clay that she said would raise the dead, mixed it with some herbs, and put it on McGrath's arm, afterward covering it with an oiled cloth which she tied on. McGrath immediately began feeling the soothing effects of the cool, wet clay.

In addition to his sons, farmer Dixon had three handsome-looking daughters, and two of them looked like they were of marrying age. Watching them working together at preparing the meal and serving it, McGrath suddenly remembered the girl he had been engaged to marry. It seemed very long ago. He was surprised to find there was no emotion left for her; neither love, nor resentment. And it was strange to realize he was no longer angry with her. He found he didn't care to think about her at all.

Then his thoughts turned to the yellow-haired girl at the restaurant, and he felt something akin to sorrow at the thought that she would never want to know him.

Before going to bed that night, he gave Dixon a map to the Flying V. On the top of the map was written, 'Flying V ranch. Owner, Vince Hamm.' He also gave the farmer a sealed letter addressed to Hamm's son, Simon, in St. Louis, informing him about the herd, apprising him of his father's situation, and telling him the Flying V was, by now, most likely overrun by Spearhead. He asked Dixon to mail the letter for him as soon as he could.

"I'll send one of the boys to town tomorrow."

One of the older Dixon boys was sent with supplies to the place where McGrath had left the Flying V livestock. The three younger boys were sent out to the barn to sleep in the hayloft and McGrath was given the bed they normally shared. He was pleased the next morning with the improvement in the way his wound looked and felt and at breakfast he thanked Mrs. Dixon for her ministrations.

She smiled and said, "We've never had to call a doctor. And look at my children. Have you ever seen a healthier bunch?"

McGrath had already observed the health of the Dixon daughters, evident in their lustrous hair, flawless complexions, slender figures, and general air of vitality. Now in the interest of giving an honest answer, he glanced at the boys and said, "No ma'am, I don't believe I have."

Before he left, he was given food for the trail and was told to come back any time. He thanked the Dixons and rode out, feeling he had made some friends, but oddly, with a heightened sense of his aloneness.

His father had told him many times, "All a man ever really owns is what he is—the kind of man he has become, good or bad. You can lose everything, but you'll always have that. So what you truly are had better be something worth having." McGrath thought of those words now and promised himself that whatever was to come, whatever he had to face, he would do it in the best way he could.

When he reached Flying V range again, he did not go back to ranch headquarters. He had completely abandoned them. He was one man alone, with no real idea of what he was going to do next. He slept in the hills that night, under a tarp, listening to the tattoo of rain on the canvas and the crash of thunder as the lightning lit up the sky. The bleak sense of loneliness he felt was as familiar as an old acquaintance. Though he was exhausted from the trail, he had difficulty falling asleep. His thoughts would not let him rest.

The rain let up in the early hours but started again around mid-morning. By that time McGrath was back in the saddle. He went to the box canyon where he had left the horses and found them still there and in good shape. The grass was almost grazed out and he knew he would have to move the animals soon. He would have to do some scouting in the wild, uninhabited places that he knew to exist in the rugged mountains no more than a day's ride away. He would move the horses in the next couple of days. He was pleased that he had been able to save all of Flying V's horses and had no intention of losing them to Spearhead.

His trail drive, on the other hand, had not been as successful. He wished he had had sufficient time and riders so that he could have done a full round-up before taking the herd off the range. As it was, he had probably saved less than a third of Flying V's cattle from being stolen by Spearhead. But at least there would be something for Vince Hamm to start over with when he got out of jail—if he got out.

The rain was still falling as McGrath started to town, and he was grateful for it. It prevented the dust that otherwise might have betrayed him to Spearhead. As he rode up the valley—still on Flying V range—he saw no cattle that bore the Flying V brand. There were, however, substantial numbers of animals bearing the Spearhead brand, and a good many of those brands were fresh. Treadwell's men had been thorough. McGrath wondered how Frank Jackson and his Double Circle were doing. Was the ranch still intact, or had Treadwell made a clean sweep?

He rode into town in the early afternoon and went straight to the courthouse where the Sheriff's office and the jail were located. The sheriff was not in the office, but one of his deputies was there, doing paperwork. McGrath said, "I'd like to see Vince."

"Can't. Sheriff Wardman won't allow it."

"Why not?"

"Ask him."

"I'm askin' you."

The deputy gave him a hard look and said, "Might have somethin' to do with the fact you're workin' for Spearhead."

"I was working for Spearhead. Now I work for Flying V."

The way the deputy said, "Uh huh," made it clear he didn't believe this. He said, "Like I said, talk to the Sheriff."

"Will you give Vince a note for me?"

The deputy nodded. McGrath asked him for a piece of paper and using a pen and inkwell that were on the desk, he wrote a very sketchy account of what he had done and the state of affairs concerning Flying V. He handed the paper to the deputy, who took it, waited for McGrath to leave, and crumpled the paper and threw it in the stove.

McGrath left the office, angry that he had not been allowed to see Vince Hamm. But as he thought about it, he was glad the Sheriff was doing all he could to protect Hamm, even if it meant that he, McGrath, would be unable to talk to his boss until after the trial. There was really nothing they needed to talk about anyway. Whatever had to be done, McGrath would have to do it alone. The trial was coming up pretty soon, and whether Hamm won his freedom or was hanged, McGrath's job would be finished then.

He walked out of the courthouse, looked down the muddy street and, thinking of the yellow-haired girl, cursed himself for a fool. He continued cursing himself for a fool as he tramped along the boardwalk to the restaurant, went in, and removed his hat and slicker, hanging them on the rack by the door.

The yellow-haired girl was walking better. Her limp was less pronounced. He liked the easy way she smiled and chatted with the customers. She had a good smile. It faded, however, when she saw him. He told himself it didn't matter—he was only there for a meal—but he knew he was lying.

She came over and poured him some coffee without asking if he

85

wanted it. "What can I get for you?" she asked in a flat tone.

He ordered steak with fried potatoes, biscuits, and gravy.

She nodded and turned away. Someone stopped her on her way to the kitchen, asking for some coffee from the pot she carried. As she poured it, her smile returned and it set up an aching within him.

Decker had been into town and had picked up the mail and some supplies. One particular letter was of great interest to him, as he knew it would be to Graham Treadwell. Back at the ranch he handed it to Treadwell, who opened and read it. "His name is Santry," Treadwell said, setting the letter on the desk behind him. Evan Santry."

"Heard of him," said Decker. "He'll do."

"Good. Ride to town tomorrow and send a telegram. I'll write it out for you."

"Is he expensive?" asked Decker, crossing a line he rarely crossed.

"Three-thousand dollars. He says we'll have to wire half of it to him before he'll even get on the train. You'll have to take care of that tomorrow, too."

Decker gave a low whistle. "Lot of money."

"It'll be worth it to get this business over and done with."

"Help me with my boots, Hughey," Jake said. He was sitting on his bed in the room he shared with his younger half-brother, who at this moment was lying in his own bed on the other side of the room, reading a book. He got up and pulled Jake's boots off for him and went back to the bed and returned to his book.

Jake sat on his bed, gazing at his half-brother, struck by the glaring differences between the two of them. Jake's mother had died when he was a baby, and a year later Graham Treadwell had married Hughey's mother. And she was the only mother Jake remembered. She had been very kind to him and he remembered feeling her loss acutely.

Hughey put down his book, sat up, and said, "You look tired."

"I am. The old man's drivin' us hard."

"I've been wanting to talk to you, Jake. I'm thinkin' of running away and I want you to come with me."

Jake was pulling off his socks. He stopped and looked squarely at Hughey. "You mean that? You're leavin'?"

"Uh huh. I haven't talked to anybody about it, but I'm plannin' on goin' to Oregon with some of the people at Canyon Mouth."

"Them nesters?"

"They're farmers, Jake."

As brothers, Jake and Hughey had a close relationship, but Jake had been raised to be a cattleman, was being groomed, in fact, to take over Spearhead someday, and certain biases in his thinking had been unavoidable.

Hughey, on the other hand, had a very different way of looking at things. "I wish you'd come with me Jake."

"How can I do that?"

"How can you not, Jake?"

"What do you mean?"

"When Pa sends the crew up to Canyon Mouth to burn those people out, he's going to expect you to be a part of that. Am I wrong?"

Jake looked down at the floor, and by not answering the question, he answered it.

"Can you do that, Jake?" persisted Hughey. "I know some of those people. They're good folks. They're my friends. And they've worked hard to build their farms. They're just tryin' to live and to raise their families. Answer me Jake, can you do it? Can you go up there and burn women and little children out of their homes? And what if some of the men decide to put up a fight—and they will—are you going to kill them?"

"They got no right to be there, Hughey. Nobody invited them."

Hughey's voice elevated in pitch, "No right?" he burst out, "That's not even Spearhead land. Spearhead is going to ride on Double Circle land and burn people out and kill them if they fight for what's theirs. What right does Spearhead have?"

Jake had no answer.

"You've got to come with me, Jake. Nobody can stop Pa from doing this, we both know that, but if you take part in it, what'll that do to us, to me and you? Those people are my friends."

Jake's head jerked up. "You would choose them over me?"

Hughey looked at him in astonishment. "How can you even ask me that Jake? It doesn't come down to who I care about most; it comes down to who's right and who's wrong. Can you defend what Pa is doing?"

Jake's answer was soft and slow in coming. "No."

"But you'll back him up. You'll ride up there and do what he tells you."

This time there was no answer. Hughey said, "You've always been a good son and you've done what you were told to do. But it was always just ranch work. This is different, and you know it. You have to decide."

There was a long interval of silence. Then Hughey said, "I wish you could know those people the way I do. Mrs. Smith, she's a widow. She's old. She's the nicest lady I've ever known. She's been teaching me how to play the piano."

Jake's eyes widened. He had not known this. "You play the piano, Hughey?"

"I'm learning."

"Are you pretty good?"

"She says I am."

"That's good, Hughey, that's real good." Jake had always looked for reasons to be proud of his little brother.

Hughey continued, "And there's the Russell family. They've got a bunch of kids and there's one daughter who's my age." He stopped, realizing he had divulged more than he had intended.

"A girl?" said Jake, grinning. "Is she your girlfriend?"

Hughey blushed. "Well, no, I wouldn't say girlfriend, but she's real nice."

Jake was not going to let Hughey off so easily. "Have you kissed her yet?"

At this moment Jake could not know how much love Hughey felt for him. It would not have been possible for him to understand what it meant to Hughey that his big brother had not acted as though the possibility of him having a girlfriend or even kissing her seemed in anyway unusual or unrealistic. And it gave strength to Hughey's hope that, despite his disfigurement, such things could be a part of his life.

Seeing the change in Hughey's countenance, but not understanding it, Jake backed off a little. "So what's her name?"

"Abby."

"Is she pretty?"

"Yes."

"Want me to go get the preacher?"

Hughey picked up a boot and threw it at his brother, who easily dodged it. They laughed for a few moments, then grew serious again, knowing that the real issue between them remained unresolved.

Like it or not, Jake had come to a crossroads in his life. They both had, but Hughey had already made his decision. He would defy his father in the only way he knew how. He would leave. With Jake, it would be different. Neither of them knew what their father would do if Jake refused to follow orders, but they both knew Jake had to be prepared for the worst. It was entirely possible that his father would throw him off the ranch and disinherit him.

"When are you leaving?" said Jake.

"I'm not sure. I'll leave when they do. It'll be soon, though."

"How old are you now, twelve?"

"I'm thirteen."

"Oh yeah."

There was a long silence and then Hughey said, "What are you thinking?"

"Just seems strange, that's all. You and I have never had anybody else, just each other. Pa, he's nothin' to us; he don't love us, and we don't love him. But the ranch . . . I sure hate the thought of leavin' this ranch."

Hughey undressed and climbed under the covers. "You have to do what's right, Jake. That's all there is. You have to do what's right."

Decker had never seen Treadwell lose control. He had seen the man angry many times but usually when Treadwell was angry he became calmer, his voice lower and more menacing. Nor did he lose complete control on this occasion, but he was very close. Close enough to raise his voice. Decker waited, saying nothing. He had been up to Canyon Mouth that day with a group of Spearhead riders and had just reported to his boss the things they had observed.

Treadwell slammed his fist on his desk, "He must have given it to them. Those farmers couldn't pay for that land. He must have just deeded it over to them."

"I guess so. The surveyor was still there and a deputy sheriff was with him keepin' an eye on things. Everyone we talked to claimed they were the legal owners of their land."

Treadwell's face was flushed, his breath came out hard. Frank Jackson and the nesters had won a battle and Treadwell was never gracious in defeat. "He's either selling them the land on installments or he's deeding it to them outright. Either way they'll have clear title."

"What do we care about that?" said Decker, "We can still run them out of the country."

"Don't be a fool, Decker," snapped Treadwell. "There are some things a man can get away with and some things that'll land him in jail."

Treadwell was silent for several minutes as he considered this latest development. Frank Jackson, the new owner of Double Circle was evidently no fool. Treadwell had not expected this ploy. The most he had expected had been a show of resistance by the farmers at Canyon Mouth. And he had had no doubt his men could easily deal with that.

Treadwell did not covet the land the nesters occupied. True, he had intended to own it and to use it as graze, but it wasn't the land itself he cared about; it was the fact that sooner or later the nesters would create their own town up at Canyon Mouth. And Treadwell wanted there to be only one town in the area and he wanted it to be his town.

He changed the subject. "Once we take over the other ranches around here, we'll have to hire more men—a lot more. Spearhead will spend a lot of money at the businesses in town and we'll be the biggest group of voters."

"Maybe then we can get rid of Wardman," said Decker. Sheriff Wardman had long been a thorn in Treadwell's side. Treadwell had been unable to influence the man with bribes or threats, and though he had tried, he had been unable to get another man elected in Wardman's place.

The town Marshall, Croft, was a different story. He was bought and paid for by Treadwell and, in town, within broad limits, Spearhead riders were relatively immune to the laws.

"We're going to have to get tougher," Treadwell said to Decker, "a lot tougher. When does Santry get here?"

"Saturday."

"Good. Put him to work right away. Let's get this thing over with."

CHAPTER 6

"It's not fair that you won't tell us, Uncle Ted," said Mandy, Frank Jackson's oldest daughter, who, like all her siblings, had called Ted Brown 'Uncle Ted,' her entire life. "He's not a young man anymore. He needs us. What if he's sick? You know he's had that stomach complaint for years." The quaver in her voice fractured and she began to cry. "We need to know."

Ted Brown was not unsympathetic, but his professional ethics would not allow him to go against the wishes of his client and he told her so. "I've been giving you his letters," he said. "What does he say? Does it sound like he's doing well?"

"He wouldn't tell us if he weren't. You know Father."

"In the last letter he sent to me," said Brown, "He said he's got some serious business to resolve and once that's taken care of he's going to come for a visit. He misses his family."

"Business?" she asked. "What does that mean? What kind of business could he possibly have at his age? He needs to be taking it easy. He needs to be enjoying life."

Brown turned and looked through the window at the distant, blue mountains, and said, "Maybe he is."

It was a large, flat area. It was perfect. Had the hills on either side of it been higher it could have been called a valley, but they were low, rounded formations and beyond them was more flat land with, here and there, another small hill.

A wide creek flowed through the middle of this area and the water table was high here. Graham Treadwell knew this because he had already had a well dug—and covered and disguised. The railroad tracks were less than a mile to the south. It was a perfect site for the town that would bear his name. And the surrounding area was perfect for that town to grow into a city.

There was one particularly large hill on the northeast side, too small to be called a mountain, but larger than any other hill around, and on this location Treadwell would build his home. The highest building in the area, it would overlook the town and its inhabitants. People would lift their eyes and gaze admiringly at it and say, "That's where Senator Treadwell lives," or perhaps it would be Governor Treadwell, or—he permitted himself the fantasy—President Treadwell.

Treadwell had spent a considerable sum of money to have the area surveyed and the streets and blocks and plots laid out and marked with iron stakes. Now, he walked down what was to be the main street, passing stakes that signified the locations of different types of businesses. He had already determined which businesses would go where. It would be a progressive city, a modern one. It would even have a bowling alley; like Tombstone.

Treadwell was pleased with the location he had chosen. It was a beautiful spot; perfect for what he had planned. It was near enough to the existing town that people who patronized the businesses there could easily come to his community where the businesses would be better and more modern, and prices would be lower—at least in the beginning. The old town would die. His town, Treadwell City, would thrive and grow.

Yes, it was a good spot. It was the perfect spot. There was only one problem. He didn't own it. Frank Jackson did.

McGrath had been gone for three days, moving the Flying V horses to another, more remote graze. Passing through town on his way back to Double Circle, he stopped in at one of the saloons for a beer. Finished, he stepped out of the saloon and walked down the boardwalk. There was a man standing by his horse and McGrath immediately recognized him as Ty Decker.

There was a sound and he turned quickly. Another man was standing behind him, his left thumb hooked behind his belt buckle and his right hand on the butt of his pistol. They had him covered on two sides. Decker was grinning now. McGrath backed up to the wall of the saloon and tried to watch them both. Who would draw first?

Decker walked around and stopped about ten feet away from the other man and folded his arms, telling McGrath by this that he was staying out of the encounter. McGrath turned his attention to the other man. Everything about this man screamed trouble. There was death in his eyes, a faint sardonic smile on his lips. He was a hired killer. McGrath was sure of it.

Decker was clearly enjoying himself. He said, "Mr. McGrath, meet Mr. Evan Santry."

Santry's lips formed a mocking smile. "Pleased." The gunman possessed an ugly, cruel face, with small eyes, a small, round mouth, a large beak of a nose and ears that stuck almost straight out from his head. He was tall with narrow shoulders and wide hips, and McGrath had heard he had killed nine men.

"McGrath's the gent that killed Guy Mustin," said Decker, his voice filled with sarcasm and contempt.

Santry emitted a disdainful snort. But he did not take his eyes off McGrath.

A door opened across the street and Marshal Croft came out. The purposeful way he walked directly over suggested that he had been watching through his window. He spoke to Decker. "Trouble?"

"No trouble, Marshal, just headin' back to Spearhead." The two men exchanged a gaze and it seemed to McGrath a message was passed to the marshal.

The marshal murmured, in a voice intended for Decker only, "Not here." He walked back across the street to the door of his office, where he turned for a moment, observing. After a moment, apparently satisfied there would be no trouble, he went into his office and closed the door.

Decker said, "You're through, McGrath. Go over to the undertaker and tell him to measure you up for a coffin." Then he went to his horse.

Santry sneered and partially turned, moving toward his own horse, always watching McGrath, never getting into a disadvantageous position.

McGrath had heard of Evan Santry, and the last thing he wanted was for a man like this to be dogging his trail. His father had taught him that business that was not taken care of early became enlarged by the delay and in the end it still had to be dealt with.

He shot a slashing glance at Decker, who had his foot in the stirrup, then back to Santry. He said, "If I ever saw a dog as ugly as you, I'd cut off its head and burn it."

Santry's hand had never left the butt of his gun, but McGrath had the advantage of knowing what was about to happen. Uttering a curse, the gunman jerked his pistol out and McGrath shot him as he raised it.

As Santry was going down, McGrath whipped his pistol around and bellowed at Decker, who was swinging into the saddle and reaching for his gun at the same time, "Don't do it, Decker."

There were people in the street now, coming out of buildings to see what the shooting was about. Decker sat there, frozen. McGrath said, "Drop your pistol on the ground." Decker did as he was told.

Behind him, McGrath heard somebody say, "He's dead."

McGrath already knew that. He knew where he had shot the man. He was no longer interested in the imported gunslinger. He said, "Carbine too, Decker."

Hatred in his eyes, Decker pulled the carbine out of the saddle scabbard and dropped it on the ground. Just then a voice shouted, "Put it down, McGrath." McGrath knew without looking that it was Marshal Croft. He holstered his gun, saying nothing.

Croft walked up to Decker, stood in front of him, and, speaking once again in a tone meant for only Decker to hear, said, "I'll handle this. Tell Treadwell I'll take care of it."

Decker picked up his guns, climbed back into the saddle, bestowed upon McGrath a long, venomous look, and rode out of town.

Croft took McGrath's gun and said, "I was watchin' through the window, McGrath. I'm a witness, and it looks like Flyin' V is going to have two murder trials."

Just then someone said in a loud voice, "Hey, ain't that Evan Santry? Why, it is, that's Santry. He's wanted. There's two-thousand dollars on his head, dead or alive."

McGrath reached out, took his pistol from the marshal's hand, and re-holstered it. "I'll be wantin' my reward, Marshal. I'll be over a little later to do the paper work so you can wire for it."

On the ride back to Spearhead, Decker had dreaded the meeting with

Treadwell. The rancher had spent fifteen-hundred dollars to bring in a hired gunfighter and McGrath had killed the man on his first day in town.

Now, standing before the incensed rancher, Decker turned his hat in his hands as Treadwell shouted obscenities. Finally, calmer, Treadwell demanded, "What happened, Decker? The two of you couldn't take McGrath?"

"McGrath's tricky. He goaded Santry. Waited 'til I had my foot in the stirrup and then prodded him into a draw."

"What did McGrath say that made Santry go for his gun?"

"Told him he was ugly."

Treadwell expelled air loudly from his lungs, closed his eyes, and shook his head in disbelief.

"Well, confound it," said Decker, "he was ugly. I guess that was what made him so touchy about it."

There was a long moment of silence while Treadwell planned his words. He said, "Lately you haven't done much of anything right, Decker. That needs to change because there are plenty of men who'd like to make the money I'm paying you. I want to make that clear."

Color rose to Decker's face. He looked down at the floor. When he looked up, he was smiling faintly, menacingly. And when he spoke, he used Treadwell's first name; something he had never done before, "Well, Graham, since we're makin' things clear, you'll want to keep in mind that I know things that could put you behind bars—put an end pronto to your high political ideas."

They glared at each other for a few moments, and Treadwell said, "There's nothing you know about me that wouldn't put you behind bars too."

"That's why we're Siamese twins. It's you and me together, all the way up the ladder or washed down the creek. Whichever way one of us goes, we go together. Let's just always remember that."

Treadwell clenched his jaw muscles for a long moment, glaring at his foreman. Finally he drew a deep breath, calming himself, and said, "That doesn't mean you can get away with not doing your job, Decker. I'll hold up my end but if you don't hold up yours the plan can't succeed. This McGrath has you buffaloed. He's trimmed your whiskers three times now, so let me tell you straight: I want him dead and I want Jackson dead. They're in my way." Then he amended, "They're in our way. Are we clear on that?"

"I think we're clear on everything, Graham."

News of the gunfight traveled like wildfire through the community. Everyone now knew that Colin McGrath was no Spearhead man. The town's collective curiosity was aroused, but there was no way to answer all the questions or put to rest the speculations and rumors that flew back and forth and around in circles like a June bug on a string, because Colin McGrath was nowhere to be found.

Flying V headquarters were abandoned. Spearhead had completely taken over Flying V's range. Vince Hamm was in jail awaiting his trial. The Flying V ranch was just a memory in the minds of those who had known it. Still, everyone wondered where McGrath had gone.

Among the most well accepted of the theories regarding McGrath's whereabouts was that he had left the area for good in search of healthier climes. Frank Jackson saw this as unfortunate. He had wanted to speak to McGrath about the two of them joining forces against Spearhead. He left word with Bonnie and Ruth to advise McGrath of his wish to speak with him should the young man turn up at the restaurant, but weeks passed and nothing happened.

Meanwhile Frank Jackson and his men spent very little time doing ranch work, owing to the fact that most of their time was spent patrolling Double Circle's boundaries to keep Spearhead at bay. Jackson himself did a good deal of night hawking, keeping close tabs on Spearhead's activities. He was constantly on the move, and he knew things were just going to get worse.

Aside from these concerns, however, Jackson felt better physically than he had in years. His chronic stomach complaint was completely gone and the constant riding had slimmed him down and taken all the flab off his waist. He was sleeping better than he had since the death of his wife and was waking up in the mornings alert and full of energy. Whenever he had a chance he wrote letters to his children and grandchildren telling them he missed them, that he was fine, and that he would soon be coming back for a visit.

On rare occasions, when he was missing his family more than usual, he questioned the wisdom in coming out here. But there was something within him that told him it had been a good decision and what he was doing was right.

In their next get-together at Bonnie's house to play cards, which, owing to circumstances, were taking place infrequently, the trio discussed Colin McGrath and the gunfight with Evan Santry.

"Well," commented Jackson, "It's pretty clear he's no longer working for Treadwell. I'd sure like to know exactly where he stands."

"You could ask him," suggested Ruth.

"I would if I could find him. He seems to have disappeared off the earth."

As it turned out, Jackson didn't have to find McGrath, McGrath found him, showing up late one night at Double Circle and being escorted in by the men who were standing guard. Hearing the riders in the yard, Jackson opened the door and, seeing that his visitor was McGrath, he invited him in.

Though it was late Jackson was fully dressed and McGrath commented, "Thought I'd find you in bed. Glad I didn't wake you."

"I've been out doin' a little night hawking myself," said Jackson.

There was a pause and Jackson waved McGrath to a chair. "Coffee?"

McGrath nodded.

Jackson went into the kitchen and brought the coffee pot and two cups. They sipped for a few moments and McGrath said, "Last time we met, we were on different sides of the fence. I just wanted to make sure you know I'm not your enemy. I've got enough to worry about with every Spearhead rider gunnin' for me, without having to worry about Double Circle, too."

"Already figured that one out," said Jackson, "Kind of makes a man curious though, how you got crosswise with Treadwell so fast."

A faint shade of embarrassment came onto McGrath's face and he said, "My Pa used to tell me it's easier to rope a wild horse than to ride it. Things look different when you're sittin' in the saddle than they did when you were standin' on the ground." He looked Jackson in the eyes, "I couldn't do what Treadwell wanted me to do."

Jackson nodded gravely. "Decker'll kill you if he gets the chance."

"Sure, sure, I know that."

There was a pause and Jackson said, "Still need a job?"

"Don't really know how to answer that. I thought I had one, but my boss is in jail, Spearhead has taken over the range, and we have no cows left except the ones I drove away."

Jackson said, "Well, since there's nothing you can do for Vince Hamm or Flying V right now, you'd be better off coming over and taking your grub here. This is getting ready to turn into a full-scale range war and I can use an extra man. You can come and go as you please. Anytime you have any Flying V business, just do it, but I think it would be best if we stuck together." Then he added, "But before you answer me let me say this. You'd be better off if you left these parts altogether. There's no real reason for you to stay that I can see."

McGrath said, "I've thought about that, but I don't even own a horse—I came into town afoot. The pony I'm ridin' belongs to Vince Hamm. It would seem kind of low to ride away on one of his horses when he's sittin' there in jail—and me, his foreman, who promised to take care of his ranch for him."

Jackson said, "I shouldn't bring this up, and you can tell me it's none of my business, but the rumor around town is you got a reward for killing Evan Santry."

"I did, but I was plannin' on lettin' Vince have that money to get a new start after he gets out of jail. He's lost all his land and most of his herd since I've been his foreman."

"That's hardly your fault."

"A man still feels a responsibility."

Jackson could see that McGrath was uncomfortable with this conversation so he changed the subject. "If it's just the horse you're worried about, I'll give you one."

"Thanks, but I liked your first offer better."

"Still stands."

"Done," said McGrath and held out his hand.

"Don't you ever get lonely?" Ruth asked Bonnie. They were sitting in the front room, resting their feet and relaxing after a long day at the restaurant.

"Not since you and Lyssa came to live with me," replied Bonnie.

"That's not what I mean. I mean your husband has been dead for years."

"Twelve years."

"Haven't you ever thought about remarrying?"

"Only a fool makes the same mistake twice, dear."

There was a pause in the conversation and then Ruth said, "I once heard a story about three young boys who wanted to go to the circus. One of them lost his money before he got there and didn't get in. One of them got in, but he got kicked by one of the horses and had to be taken to the doctor with a broken arm. The third got in, ate lots of peanuts and a candy apple, saw the show, and had a wonderful time. The next day at school the teacher asked the three boys how they liked the circus. The first boy said he didn't make it but he was going to try to see it next time it came to town. The second boy said it was awful and would never do it again. The third boy said it was the best time of his life."

Bonnie looked up from her quilting and, as was her way, leaped over the superficial comments to the heart of the matter. She said, "Are you thinking of Frank Jackson?"

"I didn't say anything about Frank," said Ruth, "but I find it interesting that you just did."

"Oh, no," said Bonnie, shaking her head. "If I'm going to walk into your trap you will at least own up to having laid it for me."

Ruth said, "What you do with your life is your business, but you can't argue that Frank is a good man and would make a good husband."

With great solemnity Bonnie reached over and patted the younger woman on the hand. "You're very young, and . . ."

Ruth interrupted. "It's true, you're older than me, but you've only been married once and so have I. And I learned everything I needed to know about my husband in the first few months of our marriage. How long did it take you to know about yours?"

Bonnie smiled and looked away. "Just a few months."

"So tell me then, what have you learned about men that I haven't?"

Bonnie did not answer the question. Instead she said, "I suppose you intend to remarry."

"Well, I'm not going to just jump at the first man that comes along, but . . ."

"You already did that," joked Bonnie, "when you asked Frank to marry you."

Ruth said in mock seriousness, "No, the Indian was the first man to come along after my husband died. I waited for the second one."

They had a long laugh, and Bonnie said, "Who knows, maybe you should have given that Indian a chance. He may have made a better husband than either of us had."

McGrath had no good excuse for coming to town and none at all for going to the restaurant. He had already eaten. He went in anyway and sat down, feeling somewhat foolish, and realized that he would have to order something. Peach cobbler sounded good so he told Ruth he would take that.

She brought it with a glass of milk. "You can't eat peach cobbler without milk," she said.

He intentionally took a long time eating and by the time he was finished, the few people that had been in the restaurant when he entered it had cleared out and the ladies were cleaning up and preparing to close.

Finished with her work, Ruth came over and sat down across from him. "My feet are killing me." She immediately regretted saying this because she had been hoping he would invite her to go for a walk with him. So, being a candid woman—and a little forward—she said, "But they're still up to walking."

Arms linked, they strolled down the street for a couple of blocks, then turned and strolled back, walking past the restaurant and down another street past Bonnie's house.

"I was married," she said irrelevantly, "to a man I didn't love."

Had she not been so direct, he would not have questioned her now. But she seemed to want to talk about this so he said, "Why did you marry him, then?"

"I was young. I'd never been in love. I thought I loved him." She paused . . . "I still believe I was in love, but I was in love with what I thought he was. And he was not at all what I thought he was."

She told him of Carl's decision for them to go to California with the wagon company, of selling all their possessions except those few they would be able to take with them, of his drinking, his abusiveness when drunk, his carelessness, his ineptitude at just about everything, and of the final sequence of bad decisions that had led to his death. She told McGrath about burying her husband, of walking for days on her broken foot, of the experience with the Indian, her escape from another, larger group of Indians, and finally, of being found by Frank Jackson.

She hesitated, then said, "I offered to marry Frank, but he turned me down."

She felt him stiffen. He slipped his arm out of hers and said, "And how long had your husband been dead?" The rebuke in his voice was unmistakable.

She had intended to tell him how foolish she now felt for having done that and to explain to him how afraid she had been at the time, but now resentment clamped her jaw shut. She would explain nothing to this man. Perhaps he did not understand fear. Perhaps he had never been afraid of anything. It occurred to her that he never would understand, and so they walked in silence to the house, where he said goodnight and she nodded and went inside.

McGrath, having no other Flying V business to attend to, often went to check on the horses and to move them from one remote, sheltered graze to another, hoping to keep them safe from Spearhead. These days, except when riding with Frank Jackson and his men, he did most of his riding at night, considering it safer. But on this night he was having doubts about that.

Quite some time ago he had begun smelling dust. He had changed his direction, trying to get away from it, but he could still smell it. He was also hearing sounds: the occasional hoof beat, a clinking of metal. Once he even thought he had heard a man's voice.

The moon was out, but the night was cloudy. Suddenly there was a break in the clouds and what he saw made his stomach clench in a knot. It was a broad semicircle of riders perhaps five-hundred yards from horn to horn and they were riding toward him.

He didn't take time to count, but he saw there were at least seven of them and he saw what they were planning and he immediately resolved not to go in the direction they wanted him to go. Cocking his pistol he spurred his horse, heading directly toward the man farthest to the right, flattening himself against the horse's neck as he rode.

They were converging on him, but most of them had farther to go than he did in order to reach that point rider and when he got close enough, he started shooting. He heard shots from the other riders, but they were a good distance away, and it was dark and he was riding fast. The chances of them hitting him were remote.

When he was close enough to the point man, he raised up in the saddle and fired his pistol two times at the man's horse and saw it drop. A few seconds later he was past and riding away into the darkness. As he rode he reloaded his pistol and holstered it, slipping the thong over the hammer. He could not afford to lose the gun.

He was headed toward a straight-sided butte with a wide defile in it. When he got to the defile he entered it, wishing he knew this country better. These men had a definite advantage over him when it came to knowledge of the terrain.

He came out of the defile on the far side and was met by a series of rolling hills. In the bright moonlight he saw a narrow creek that flowed through the valley between two of these hills. He crossed it and continued on toward a higher set of bluffs. There were trees there and the promise of a hiding place. It seemed the obvious place to go and for this reason he resisted its call and rode in a different direction. Soon he heard hoof beats behind him and he ducked into a gully, ground tied the horse and climbed up to the top of a low hill, lying flat on his stomach and peering over.

They were bunched in a group, close enough that he could hear voices and make out a word now and then. One of them pointed and shouted, "He'll be up in those trees. Spread out."

McGrath felt the need to be on his way, but his horse was tired and he wanted the Spearhead men to be too far away to smell his dust when he did move. He stayed where he was for nearly an hour, then checked his cinch and stepped into the saddle.

He rode all night, stopping to rest the horse occasionally, and by morning he was in country that was completely unfamiliar to him. Fatigue was pulling at his muscles and there was a temptation to find a place to sleep for an hour or two. But this was not the first time McGrath had been hunted. Not so very long ago he had been in similar circumstances and had survived because he had never underestimated his enemies. When it had seemed logical that his pursuers had stopped pursuing he had continued, behaving as though they still were. When it had seemed safe to stop and rest he had refrained from doing so.

And so he pushed himself and his tired horse throughout the day, and later that day he saw dust in the distance behind him. By intention, he took his course into an increasingly rugged country, broken by deep canyons and ravines and up-thrust ramparts, wooded in some places and in others too barren for trees.

Night came and he rested his horse for a couple of hours but did not allow himself the dangerous luxury of sleeping. When sunrise came he had been back on the trail for hours. He saw no hint of pursuit and once again the temptation was strong to get some sleep. But again he resisted.

When he saw the distant dust at midmorning it occurred to him that these men were not just following orders. They were after a reward. He now had no doubt that Treadwell had put a bounty on his head; otherwise, those riders would have given up the previous day.

As the day wore on, his physical fatigue dragged his emotions down into discouragement and depression, making the world appear an ugly and dirty place and life pointless and hard. And he felt his old sense of hostility toward the human race begin to resurface. Loneliness seemed to do that to him.

Darkness came. He had been following a distinct trail for some time and so, at about midnight, hoping his pursuers would expect him to stay on that same trail, he left it and rode a few miles away to where he stopped to let his horse rest and graze and to allow himself a couple hours of necessary sleep. It was dawn the next morning when from the top of a hill, he watched the riders pass. He waited until they were well past, then ran to his horse and saddled it.

The sleep had refreshed him somewhat, but lack of food was beginning to tell. He swung into the saddle and turned the horse back toward Double Circle. It was in his mind that the Spearhead riders would expect him to continue riding away, not back in the direction from which they had come.

Dawn came and the sky was cloudy. He was taking care to avoid raising too much dust. At some point, now that daylight had come, he knew the Spearhead riders would realize they had lost him and would backtrack, and they would pick up his trail and follow it. His hope was that he could be far enough away by the time they did that they could never catch him.

It was about eight o'clock in the morning when it began to rain. The night of rest and food had done his horse good and now that there was no risk of raising dust, he pushed the horse harder.

He rode all day, stopped briefly that night for a rest and to graze his horse, and then rode the rest of the night, finally arriving at town around noon the following day, having seen no sign of his pursuers for the past two days.

He tied his horse behind the restaurant and went in through the back door. Bonnie saw him come in and said with her usual candor, "Mr. McGrath, you look terrible. Frank has been worried about you. Where have you been?"

Pulling off his hat, he said, "Ma'am if you'd feed me and find me a quiet place to lie down for a few hours, I'll tell you the whole story."

She fed him and afterward said, "I don't know that I've ever seen a human being wolf down a meal that fast."

He stood up, and she could see the fatigue pulling his features down, rounding his shoulders. She said, "Go to my house. It's unlocked. There are two bedrooms upstairs. Take either one of them. I'll have Tom Lee take care of your horse."

"Thank you, Ma'am," he said and shuffled out the door.

Of the men who had originally started pursuing McGrath, only three made it back to Spearhead range as a group. One of them, tired of the chase, had refused to go on after the second day and Decker had fired him on the spot and sent him back to the ranch to collect his pay.

Another, on the ride back, had fallen out of the saddle onto the ground, utterly exhausted. Decker had unsaddled the man's horse and left it there grazing, while its rider lay on the ground asleep.

Now, back on Spearhead, Decker dreaded the thought of facing Treadwell and having to admit that once again McGrath had beaten him. They had picked up his trail earlier that day and followed it to the point where it turned toward town. Here, Decker had to decide whether to abandon the chase and return to Spearhead, or follow McGrath to town.

When he made his decision and reined his horse toward town, one of the riders hung back and said, "What are you doin', Decker?"

Decker turned and squared himself against the dissenting rider. "Somethin' you want to say?"

"Not a thing." The man turned and rode away.

Too fatigued to argue, Decker turned to his last rider and said, "How about you Robart?"

Robart was a member of Decker's hardened crew who had attached himself, leech-like, to Decker. He was a man of little intelligence, ambition, or originality of thought, but he had no scruples and he saw in Ty Decker a man who, if obeyed, could be a steady meal ticket for him. Bone weary as he was now, he shrugged, "Might as well see it through."

McGrath's trail led to the back of the restaurant and from there Decker could see where the horse had been led away by someone on foot. They followed it to the livery stable. McGrath was not there.

"Must be in the restaurant," said Decker.

They rode around to the street and back down to the restaurant where they dismounted and walked inside. McGrath was not there either. Back outside they mounted and rode around again to the back of the restaurant. Decker again dismounted, walked in through the back door, and looked around.

"Something I can do for you?" said Bonnie indignantly.

Decker did not acknowledge her; he checked the storeroom and then left the building. The privy and shed out back were empty as well. The two men rode toward Spearhead, but about a half mile out of town Decker stopped and said, "He's got to be at her house."

No one was around when the two men rode up to the house and got off their horses. "Take off your spurs," said Decker, and he did the same. The front door was unlocked and they entered, going quietly from room to room. There was no one in any of the rooms on the ground floor.

Carefully they took the stairs and found McGrath sleeping soundly in one of the upstairs bedrooms. He had removed his gun belt but not his boots. Decker had his pistol out. He put it against McGrath's head.

McGrath woke instantly and Decker swung the pistol viciously against his skull. McGrath was not completely knocked unconscious, but he was dazed. They dragged him downstairs and tied him across the saddle of one of the horses. Decker said to Robart, "You can walk."

"I can't walk all the way to Spearhead."

"We ain't goin' to Spearhead," said Decker.

"Where then?"

"Up to the Crazy Horse. The back entrance."

Robart looked confused for a moment and then a wicked grin came onto his face.

The Crazy Horse mine had been closed down for months. There was constant talk of reopening it, but so far nothing had happened. It was a steep ride up to the mine, with frequent switchbacks in the road. McGrath twisted his hands, trying to loosen the ropes that bound them, but he was securely tied.

During the ride Decker kept a constant watch to make sure they were not seen, and when they finally reached the opening, he was convinced they had not been. Before untying his captive, Decker once again slammed the pistol barrel against his head, opening a gash on the side of his forehead. And when they loosened the rope, McGrath dropped to the ground, blinking his eyes rapidly, shaking his head in an attempt to clear it.

They half dragged, half carried him into the mine. A wooden barricade had been constructed to keep children from getting in, but someone had removed part of it, creating an opening. Decker knew that a lot of the young boys from town liked to come up here to drop rocks into the shaft. He and Robart dragged McGrath through the opening. Decker lit a match and said, "Alright now, be careful Robart. It's thirteen-hundred feet down."

This seemed to clear McGrath's head. He tried to stand up and Decker delivered another solid blow to his head with the pistol barrel, cursing him fiercely. McGrath lay immobile, and Robart gave him several vicious kicks to the ribcage and head and said, "Let's do it, Decker." He pulled his pistol and said, "Let's shoot him now."

Decker said, "No. I want him to know. I want him to feel it all the way down. We'll wait 'til he comes to."

It took a few minutes for McGrath to revive. When he did, they hoisted him to his feet, standing him at the very edge of the shaft. Then Decker said, "McGrath?"

"What?"

"Say your prayers. It's a long way to the bottom."

McGrath had been hit so many times on the head that his thoughts were fuzzy and uncontrolled. He knew he was in serious trouble but wasn't sure what he could do about it. His legs felt weak and rubbery, his sense of balance tentative. He knew that without the man on either side supporting him, he would fall. He felt an intense sense of danger.

He heard Decker laugh and then he felt a shove from behind and he fell forward. He instinctively put out his hands to catch himself, but there was nothing there. Suddenly his brain was much clearer and he understood that he was falling and falling and falling.

Pointing his pistol down into the shaft, Robart began firing. Decker bellowed, "Stop it, you fool!"

"Why?"

"I wanted to hear him hit bottom. Now I can't hear anything. I'm practically deaf. Don't you know you can't shoot a gun inside a mine?" He paused at the edge of the shaft and then turned and said, "Let's go. I'm hungry and I'm tired."

They left the mine, squinting their eyes against the brightness of the sun, and rode down the steep haul road. At the bottom they turned their horses toward Spearhead.

CHAPTER 7

"What?" said Treadwell, scarcely able to believe what he had just heard. "You got him? Avery came back earlier and said you hadn't"

"We got him. We got McGrath."

"Where is he?"

"He's dead."

"Where'd you leave him?"

Decker grinned. "We threw him down a shaft up at the Crazy Horse."

"A deep one, I hope," said Treadwell.

"Thirteen-hundred feet deep enough for you?"

It was the first time Decker had seen Treadwell smile in a very long time and it made him feel that he had finally redeemed himself after a string of failures. "I told you I'd get him, Boss. I always do."

He told Treadwell the full story and Treadwell said, "Go get yourself some rest, and then I want Jackson out of the way."

"Jackson," sneered Decker, "He ain't nothin'."

"Then it shouldn't take as long as it did with McGrath."

As Decker started to turn away, Treadwell said, "I like the Crazy Horse plan. You say that's thirteen-hundred feet?"

"Uh huh."

"Alright then, that'd be a real nice place for Jackson."

Decker nodded and as he shambled to the door, Treadwell said, "That's deep enough even their stink can't get out."

Though he was almost entirely ignored by his father and by Decker and most of his crew, Hughey knew a lot about what went on around the ranch. It wasn't that he was very inquisitive about ranch business; in fact, the reverse was true, but he had a quick mind and even without caring much about it he was able to piece things together by observing the actions of the crew and by bits of conversation he accidentally picked up here and there.

Tonight, however, it was not bits of conversation he overheard; it was the entire story. He was sneaking out as he often did, had come down the stairs, and was passing the doorway to the front room, headed for the kitchen, from where he would take the back door out. But he stopped when he heard Decker announce that McGrath was dead. Shrinking into the darkness, Hughey listened to the entire conversation. And when Decker went out the front door, Hughey slipped out the back.

Earlier that evening when the crew was at supper and no one was watching, he had saddled a horse and hid it in a particular spot that he generally used for that purpose. His plan was to go up on Silent Mountain and spend a couple of nights camping out, cooking his meals over a campfire. He would lie on his back and watch the stars and be awake early to see the sunrise from that particularly advantageous spot, as he had done many times before.

Hughey's plan changed, however, when he heard what Decker had done to Colin McGrath. It was a well-known fact around the ranch and up at Canyon Mouth that McGrath was working with Frank Jackson of the Double Circle. Hughey considered these people to be his friends and his father, Ty Decker, and his crew of hard cases to be his enemies. Therefore, instead of riding to Silent Mountain, he spurred his horse toward the Double Circle.

"It doesn't make sense," Ruth said. She and Bonnie were standing in the room where McGrath had gone to sleep. "He wouldn't have left his gun belt."

"You're right," agreed Bonnie. "Where would he have gone? Where could he have gone without a horse?"

Tom Lee had already been sent to the livery stable and had returned with the news that McGrath's horse was still there and that McGrath had not been seen.

"It just doesn't make sense," repeated Ruth. "Something's happened to him."

About that same time there was a knock at the door of the Double Circle ranch house. Hughey had been seen by Jackson's sentries but was allowed to pass. Jackson looked out through a slit in the shutters and, seeing it was Hughey, opened the door.

Breathlessly Hughey said, "I've got somethin' bad to tell you."

Frank Jackson stood in front of the door of the small shack and rapped lightly on it, wondering what kind of reception he would receive at four o'clock in the morning. He soon found out. He heard sleepy cursing from within and presently a hairy-chested man wearing pants and galluses but no shirt or shoes opened the door. "Yeah?"

"I'm looking for Perry Strickland," said Jackson. "I was told I would find him here."

"Strickland," shouted the man and turned away from the door and disappeared.

Shortly thereafter another man came to the door. This one was short and slender and wiry, with a narrow face and a pointed jaw. He appeared to be in his mid-twenties and when he spoke there was no mistaking the accent. "What can I do for you, sir?"

"Mrs. Ames told me you might be interested in doing a day of work." Mrs. Ames was the woman to whom Jackson took his clothes to be laundered. She knew everyone in town and all their business and was a consummate gossip. Jackson had woken her to ask her if she knew of someone trustworthy who knew the Crazy Horse mine well.

"Mrs. Ames was right. I've been out of work since the mine closed," said Strickland. "What kind of work is it?"

"Get your clothes on and come out. We'll talk."

Outside, a few minutes later, Jackson said, "I need a man: a miner who knows the Crazy Horse and can keep his mouth shut."

"That sounds like me."

"Good. A friend of mine was thrown into a shaft up there. I want you to help me retrieve his body. I want to give him a decent burial and I want proof that he was murdered. I'm going to try to bring the people who did it to justice."

"Which shaft did they throw him in?"

"I'm not sure. All I know is that you get to it from the opening on the back side of the mountain and it's about thirteen-hundred feet deep."

Strickland nodded. "I helped drill that shaft." He stroked his chin and said, "I might or might not be able to help you."

"Depending on what?" asked Jackson.

"How high the water's got. You can't go down thirteen-hundred feet on a rope. There's only so far down that I'd go that way even if you could. When the mine was running, we used cables and winches, but you and I won't have that kind of equipment."

Jackson said, "I thought we could get to the bottom parts of the shaft from one of the lower levels."

"No. The lower levels are already flooded, so we couldn't use them to get to that particular shaft." He was pensive for a moment, then he said, "But it wouldn't matter anyway because the shaft would be flooded to the same level they are. The body will be floating, so if the water's high enough, we won't have to go too far down to get it. What we need to know is how far up the water has risen. Why don't we go up there and have a look?"

"That's fine."

"I don't have much equipment," said Strickland, "but I can gather a couple of hats and candle spikes and plenty of rope. I'll have to have some breakfast first and I'll need a little time to round up the things we need. Can you meet me here in two hours?"

Jackson nodded. "Alright." And he added, "Let's don't tell anyone about this just yet." He extended his hand and Strickland took it. As he gripped the miner's hand, Jackson became aware that part of it was missing.

Strickland said, "I lost the two fingers in a mine accident. They almost didn't let me come back to work, but I proved I can still do the work as well as any other man."

Jackson went to the restaurant and had breakfast, attempting to act natural. He did not tell Ruth and Bonnie what Hughey had told him about McGrath's death. That could wait.

Decker was the kind of foreman who liked to know everything that went on around the ranch. He knew about Hughey's little trips. He knew when he was gone, and he generally knew where he went. He knew about the spot where Hughey hid his horse for a quick escape and he usually knew when the boy came back home. It amused him to know these things, and it amused him even more to know that he knew more about Hughey's doings than the kid's father did.

He had never considered Hughey to be any kind of threat, but tonight when he and Treadwell had been talking, Decker had thought he heard a sound by the door into the kitchen. And so before staggering off to bed, he sent one of the hands to follow the boy. "Find out where he goes and what he does and then come back and tell me. But don't wake me until mornin'."

Next morning upon receiving the news that the boy had gone directly and hastily to Double Circle, Decker went immediately to the main house and told Treadwell of his son's betrayal.

It pleased Decker to see the fire of anger in Treadwell's eyes. For a long time he had wanted to see that boy get a good whipping. Decker was also pleased that this was something that could not be blamed on him. He had done everything right. It was Treadwell's own laxity with his son that had caused this.

Treadwell said, "We can make this work in our favor."

"How's that?"

"If Jackson goes up to the mine to try to find McGrath's body, and you are there waiting . . ." He left the rest unspoken and Decker understood. Jackson's body could join McGrath's at the bottom of that shaft. Another enemy of Spearhead would be out of the way and there would be no way for anyone to pin it on Spearhead.

He nodded and smiled, and though it was a lie he said, "I was just thinkin' the same thing myself." Abruptly he broke into a run, charged past the amazed Treadwell and through the doorway to the kitchen. Treadwell heard two sets of boots on the stairway and then a cry of pain. Presently Decker appeared, dragging Hughey along.

He thrust the boy at his father who caught him with both hands. Decker said, "That's twice, Graham."

Grinning sadistically, Decker watched as Treadwell in uncontrolled rage beat his son. It surprised Decker that Hughey didn't scream or beg or even cry out. He took the beating silently, raising his hands to ward off the blows, but in no other way defending himself.

At length, breathing heavily from exertion and anger, Treadwell said to Decker, "Get him upstairs. Lock the door from the outside—and I want his window nailed shut."

As Decker lifted Hughey to his feet, Treadwell came and stood in front of his son and with a voice as calm as death and as hard as flint, he spoke the cruelest words he could think of. "You're worthless, just like your worthless mother, and you always will be. You may no longer consider yourself to be my son."

Decker took the boy upstairs and locked him in his room, then went out and gave orders for the window to be nailed shut. He chose two men to go with him and as soon as the horses were saddled they rode out. As they approached the mine, Decker saw two horses tied outside the west tunnel.

He grinned and said to Robart, "Jackson moves fast. This is going to be easier than I thought."

Jackson's candle did little to illuminate the dark shaft and he could see no great distance down into the hole. He dropped a rock down the shaft and counted how long it was before he heard it hit the water.

Turning to Strickland he said, "Two seconds, maybe a little more. That's not very far down."

"No," said Strickland, "This mine is filling up fast."

The story, as it had been relayed to Jackson by Hughey, was that McGrath had been shot before being dumped in the shaft. Jackson wanted to believe there was hope that McGrath could be alive, but even if the water was high enough that the impact hadn't killed him, and even if he had not died from being shot but had survived his wounds, he had spent all night in freezing water. That he could have survived all that was simply too much to be hoped for.

Nevertheless, Jackson shouted down the shaft, "McGrath, are you there?"

At first he thought he was imagining it, but a sound came up from below, the definite sound of a human voice. Jackson felt his pulse quicken, "McGrath, is that you?"

"Yes." The voice was weak.

"Judging by where the water is," said Strickland, "he's a ways below the next level down. We need to get to the level below this one and try to get to him from there."

Strickland secured the end of a rope to one of the iron haulage tracks that ran along the floor of the tunnel, then threw the rope over the side. "Can you do this?" he asked Jackson.

"Sure," said Jackson. "I'm not so old I can't climb down a rope. Climbing back up, well . . . that may be a different story."

Strickland went first and when he called up that he was at the next level, Jackson lowered the canvas bags containing their equipment and afterward went cautiously over the side, grateful for the leather gloves he had brought.

The next level was a tunnel much like the one they had just left, except that it did not communicate with the outside. Jackson looked around the level, his eyes now adjusted to the dim light provided by the candle on the candle spike he wore on his hat. He leaned out and called McGrath's name again. The voice was still as weak, but it sounded closer. "How far down are you?" asked Jackson.

Strickland said, "He can't know that." He secured another rope to one of the rails on this level and tossed it down. "Did you hear that?" he shouted.

"Yes," came the weak reply.

"Can you get hold of it?"

Jackson, holding the rope, felt McGrath grasp it from below.

"Take hold of the rope and we'll pull you up."

"Can't," said McGrath, "too weak."

"Can you tie it around your waist?"

It was a long time before the reply came back, "Can't. Hands don't work."

They looked at each other and Strickland voiced what they were both thinking, "He's in bad shape. I'll go down the rope and tie him on. I'll come back up and we'll pull him up together. He'll be dead weight. It'll take both of us to do it."

Jackson nodded. As quickly as a sailor, Strickland went down the rope and soon Jackson could make out the sounds of the two men talking. He felt the movements of the rope as Strickland tied it around McGrath.

"I'm coming up," Strickland shouted.

Jackson watched as Strickland's candle started up the rope and soon the man's face was in view. Jackson helped him over the rim and, dripping wet and breathing heavily, Strickland said, "Your man's almost dead. He might not make it. We've got to warm him up."

As they pulled McGrath up, Strickland said, "He's been lying on a little shelf of rock, but his clothes were wet. I had to get in the water to tie the rope on him."

When they got McGrath up, Jackson could see that what Strickland had told him was no overstatement. McGrath's lips were blue, his eyes deep sunk. He lacked the strength to stand and could barely speak.

They laid him on the floor and immediately began removing his sodden clothes. Jackson started to say something when a voice from above called out his name.

"Jackson, hey you down there; got a little present for you." The rope that was their only connection to safety came sailing down the shaft. "Enjoy yourself down there, Jackson. It's a nice, bright, sunny day outside."

They heard Decker laugh.

Jackson and Strickland stood looking at each other. Jackson said, "Does this tunnel lead out?"

"No. It's a dead end."

"I'll leave a couple of men up here," shouted Decker, "to make sure you don't figure out a way to climb up. I'll leave 'em here for a while, Jackson. In fact, they'll be here for the rest of your life." He laughed again. And then they heard no more from Decker.

Strickland moaned, "This is bad. This is very bad. We'll die here."

"Let's worry about that later," said Jackson. "Is there any wood around here?"

"Sure, timbers. A mine's full of wood."

"Get me some to make a fire. We've got to warm both of you up."

Jackson finished removing McGrath's clothing, which he laid aside. He then removed his own outer clothes and put them on McGrath.

They soon got a fire going, and Strickland stood near it, warming himself and drying his clothes while Jackson massaged McGrath's feet and hands. The fire was a big one and the tunnel grew uncomfortably warm for Jackson, but he made no complaint, knowing the other two needed the heat. The smoke from the fire was drawn out into the shaft and upward. From there, Jackson did not know where it went.

As he grew warmer, McGrath seemed to revive to a degree and presently he was able to sit up and lean back against the wall of the tunnel while Jackson set about drying his clothes.

This accomplished, he and McGrath exchanged clothes again and McGrath, now able to speak, said, "You shouldn't have come, Frank."

Jackson had earlier introduced him to Strickland and McGrath now said, "I'm sorry, Strickland."

Strickland replied, "What's done is done. A bloke does what he thinks is right and takes his blows."

Jackson had brought some beef jerky, and this he gave to McGrath who needed it most. They sat by the fire for several hours while McGrath ate jerky and soaked up the warmth, growing visibly stronger. During this entire time they heard the sound of rocks periodically being thrown down the shaft and plopping in the water. Decker had obviously left a man behind, and this man was either tossing rocks to pass the time or was doing it to make sure the men trapped below knew he was there.

Jackson said, "McGrath, we were told you were shot before they threw you down the shaft."

McGrath shook his head, "No. I heard shots while I was falling, but I don't know if they were shooting at me or not. I guess they must have been."

"How do you feel?" asked Jackson.

"Weak as a kitten, but it's nice to be warm."

Jackson turned to Strickland and said, "I don't plan on sitting here until I die. There has to be something we can try. Think, man, you know this mine. We know what's above us and that's out of the question. Tell me what's below us."

"Nothing that's not under water."

"How far under water is the next level?" asked Jackson.

"Probably not more than ten feet."

"If we were to get to the next level, would we be able to swim to another shaft?"

Strickland seemed to contemplate this for a long time. "Maybe."

"If we got to another shaft, could we get out of the mine?"

"Not without a winch and a bucket to hoist us up. The next shaft goes up as far as this one goes down."

There was silence now and they let it run on for twenty minutes or more, soaking up the warmth of the fire, immersed in their own thoughts. Finally McGrath said, "We know we can't get out through this tunnel or the shaft. I say we try to get to the next one and figure out what to do when we get there. At least there won't be somebody with a gun there waiting to shoot us if we make a try for it."

"I agree," said Jackson. "We can't just sit here and die."

Strickland did not speak; he merely sat staring at the fire. Finally Jackson said, "Strickland, how do you feel about this?"

Strickland looked up and said, "It won't work, but I can't think of a better idea, so we may as well try it."

They planned everything very carefully. Strickland hadn't brought a lot of equipment, but he had brought plenty of rope and so the plan was for Jackson, who claimed to be a good swimmer, to dive down, find the tunnel and swim to the next shaft with a rope attached to him. Using a system of signals they devised, consisting of different numbers of pulls on the rope, they would communicate. If Jackson got into trouble, he would signal so, and they would pull him back—hopefully in time to save him from drowning. If he made it through, he would pull the other two through one at a time.

Strickland dripped some candle wax onto a few matches to waterproof them and gave these and a candle to Jackson. "Don't lose them," he admonished. "I'll wax all of them while I'm at it."

Jackson nodded. He understood the importance of light in this blackness.

"There are plenty of things to snag your clothes on," said Strickland, "and if you get snagged on something, you'll drown, so be careful."

Jackson thought about this for a moment and then stripped off his clothes. "I'll swim faster without them dragging me down. You two had better do the same."

"Good idea," agreed Strickland. McGrath and I will do the same.

McGrath groaned.

They stuffed all their supplies and clothing into the canvas bag and tied a rope around it.

"How cold's the water?" asked Jackson as he stood there preparing to make his dive.

"Cold enough," said Strickland.

He was right. The shock of the water almost made Jackson expel the deep lungful of air that he had taken in just before diving. He felt the pressure build up against his eardrums as he kicked and pulled his way deeper. There was no visibility down here. It was completely dark. He had to feel his way along the side of the shaft. When he came to the tunnel he immediately knew he had found it and he entered it, kicking with his feet and feeling his way forward with his hands. Once he blundered into a timber, striking his head on it. His lungs were already screaming for air, and he knew he was nowhere near the shaft.

He pushed himself upward until he touched the ceiling of the tunnel with his hands, searching for any trapped pocket of air that might be there. His muscles ached, his lungs screamed for air. He knew he was not going to make it.

Then one of his hands broke the surface. He felt the air. He turned his face upward, pushing it up against the rock, reaching the trapped air, gulping it into his burning lungs.

He remained there for at least a minute, paddling with his hands and feet to keep his face in the small space between the surface of the water and the roof of the mine. Finally he drew in several deep breaths and held the last one, ducked his head under, and continued. He stayed close to the ceiling, partly because he hoped for another air pocket, but primarily because this would be how he would know when he was in the next shaft. And with his lungs once again near to bursting, he felt the ceiling go away and he pushed himself upward, at last breaking the surface. The darkness here was complete.

His hand struck something on the surface and it felt like a tree. He immediately knew it was a timber. He laid his arms across it, bent at the elbows, and allowed the buoyancy of the timber to take his weight while he rested and caught his breath. Presently, as his muscles took on new oxygen and rested from the strain, he felt stronger and he kicked with his feet, pushing himself and the timber forward until it was against the wall of the shaft. Now he pulled on the rope three times; the signal that he had made it. Strickland pulled back, acknowledging.

The candle and the matches were still tightly gripped in Jackson's hand, and with trembling fingers, he struck a match on the hard rock, lit the candle, and took a look around. There were several more timbers floating in this chamber, enough in fact to support a man. The big question now was if McGrath and Strickland came over and joined him here would they be any better off than they had been where they were?

He held the candle aloft and looked above. He could see the next level, but could a man climb up to it? The walls of the shaft were far from being smooth. There were depressions and outcroppings that could afford handholds and footholds for an agile man. Jackson was a big man. It was not a job for him. It would either have to be McGrath or Strickland. And Jackson wasn't sure if McGrath was up to the job yet. Then he remembered Strickland's hand. The man was able to grip a rope, but clinging to tiny outcroppings of rock required more than three fingers. He experienced a feeling of hopelessness.

Pushing it away, he spent a good ten minutes working on wedging some of the floating timbers across the shaft in such a way that they would not easily move and afterwards hoisted himself to a sitting position upon them. He set the candle on a tiny shelf of rock just above his head and gave the signal. He soon received the answering signal and began pulling on the rope with all his strength, knowing that Strickland would be unable to breathe until he broke the surface in this chamber. He admired the man's guts. A man who does not know how to swim is generally afraid of being in the water. Strickland was putting a lot of faith in Jackson and Jackson pulled for all he was worth.

Sooner than he expected, Strickland broke the surface, spitting and gasping and cursing. Jackson pulled him to the timber and the Cornishman grabbed hold of it, throwing his arms over the top of it. "Never again," he said, "I will never do that again, if I have to rot down here."

They pulled their equipment through, gave the signal to McGrath, and received his answering signal that he was ready. McGrath's trip, like Strickland's, was uneventful, but unlike Strickland, he had nothing to say after breaking the surface. He merely swam over to the timbers and laid his arms across them, laying his head to one side. Jackson had a sense of how sick and weary the man must be. He said, "How are you doing, McGrath?"

Through chattering teeth, McGrath said, "Fine, Frank. Doin' fine."

"Get up out of the water. We'll help you."

The three naked men sat for a few minutes on the timbers, shivering, their teeth chattering, and then Jackson said, "Let's get these timbers lashed together. We need some kind of a base here." Reluctantly he slid back into the water and, working together, the men soon had the timbers lashed into a flat, somewhat stable surface, measuring the length of the timbers by about six feet in width.

Finished, they placed their bag of supplies on it and lay there on their backs, resting and shivering.

"The answer is no," said Bonnie. "Absolutely not. Come here, Lyssa. Sit on Grandma's lap."

Lyssa ran over to where Bonnie was sitting and climbed up on the woman's lap, giggling as Bonnie kissed her on the neck. Then, settling the child on her lap, Bonnie said, "There's absolutely no need for it. It's foolishness. I have all this room here and I'm alone. I have adopted Lyssa as my granddaughter and if you try to take her away, I will steal her from you and she and I will find a cave to live in where you won't find us and you'll never see either of us again." She tickled the squirming child.

Ruth laughed. "I just feel like we're imposing on your kindness."

"Oh, you are; it's terrible. You do most of the housework. You do most of the cooking and, as you can see, I can't tolerate your awful child. I don't know how I've stood it this long."

Gravely, Ruth said, "She's not my child, Bonnie. We must not forget that."

Bonnie sobered and nodded, and during the ensuing silence she stroked Lyssa's hair and squeezed her so tightly that the girl finally squeaked in complaint.

Bonnie said to Ruth, "Don't worry, dear, I know it's not permanent. Pretty as you are, it's only a matter of time before some handsome young fellow comes to the restaurant and sees you and carries you off. And I'll be happy for you when that happens. Meanwhile we have a good arrangement. I like it and I think it works for you too. So why change it?"

"Well then," said Ruth, "at least let me pay you some rent."

"Absolutely not. There is no reason for it. But, I'll tell you what I will do: The next time you marry, don't marry a poor man. Hold out for a rich husband, and I'll give him the bill for all your back rent."

Ruth laughed again. "There's just one hole in your plan."

"And what's that?"

"What if some handsome, older fellow comes along and carries you off?"

"I can't see that happening, can you?"

"Why not?"

Bonnie shook her head. "You know how I feel about men."

Ruth had a swift desire to tell Bonnie she was a fraud. Since she had been working with the woman, she had become aware of the fact that anyone who was down on their luck could always get a free meal at Bonnie's restaurant. And every cowboy in the area knew that if he needed to borrow money, he could go to Bonnie with a hard luck story and get it. Ruth refrained from mentioning any of this, however. She said, "I know how you profess to feel about men. I can only guess as to the real truth."

"No, my dear, I made that mistake once. Never again."

"I made a mistake the first time, too," said Ruth, "That doesn't mean the next time can't be different for either of us."

There was a long silence as Bonnie rocked Lyssa, who was falling asleep, and Ruth mended a tear in one of the child's dresses. The clock on the wall ticked loudly in the silence, the burning wood in the stove in the kitchen made a sound as it settled, Lyssa's breathing became rhythmic as she fell asleep.

Ruth finally said, "I can hardly stand it."

Knowing exactly what she was talking about, Bonnie said, "How will we let her go? How will we be able to bear that?"

"I think about that and then I think of her poor mother who must be frantic with worry and grief."

She put down her mending and went over and kissed the sleeping child. She said, "I've sent eight letters just this last week. The way I keep sending them, you'd think I was anxious to be rid of her."

"You're just trying to do the right thing, dear. Some people are like that and you're one of them."

"I'm not that good, Bonnie. Every time I send a letter a part of me hopes it doesn't arrive."

"I know," said Bonnie, "Me too."

They sat for a time in silence as their thoughts were centered on this worrisome matter. Finally, Ruth said, "I wonder why Frank hasn't stopped by."

"He must be very busy," said Bonnie.

Decker knocked on the front door of the house and a husky female voice called out from within. "Who's there?"

"Me. Open up."

A thick, blocky woman in her sixties opened the door. She had dirty-blonde hair the texture of dried grass and an unlovely face that very much resembled Decker's. If there had ever been a smile on that face or a look of compassion in the eyes, they had left no traces in their passing.

Decker brought in two flour sacks filled with supplies. The woman waved a hand toward a table and Decker set the sacks on it and said, "I got everything on your list."

"Did you bring my pay?"

He withdrew an envelope from his shirt pocket and handed it to her. She opened it and counted the money.

"All there?" he asked sardonically.

"Little as it is," she said. "Did you tell him I want more?"

"Uh huh."

"And what happened?"

"Me telling him and him doing it are two different things, Ma."

"Maybe he thinks this is fun, sitting here day after day and never being able to go anywhere."

"It's what you agreed to when you took the job, and he pays you good money. You make almost as much as I do."

"I need a helper," she insisted. "Someone who could stay here sometimes and let me have a chance to get away."

Decker took her by the arm and pulled her outside. "No, Ma," he stated flatly. "He won't hear of it. There are three people in the world who know about her: you and me and him. He only trusted you because you're my mother and you know the kind of trouble we'd all be in if anybody found out."

"How long does this have to go on?" she asked.

"I don't know, but Treadwell is going to rise, and I'm going to rise with him. Someday that will mean a lot to you and me. He says the public can accept a widower, even feel sorry for him. Some people will vote for him just because they feel bad that he lost his wife. But a man with a crazy wife will lose votes. People don't like that. They don't like the sound of it. Some folks may even think she went crazy because of him."

Decker's mother snorted. "Crazy! She's no more crazy than I am."

He waved this away with his hand. "Well, it's too late to tell that to anyone, Ma. She's been here too many years now. Just hold on a little longer. A lot of things are gettin' ready to change."

CHAPTER 8

Jackson held his candle aloft, his eyes traveling upward along the rough wall of the shaft where he and McGrath and Strickland sat shivering. Looking at the dimly seen opening to the next level, he dreaded what he was about to ask. "McGrath, are you good at climbing?"

"Sure," said McGrath, knowing what was being asked of him. "I'll do it."

Jackson glanced at Strickland, who gave him a concerned look, and said, "Alright, tie another rope around you."

Standing unsteadily on the timbers, McGrath wrung out his pants and shirt and put them on. He emptied the water out of his boots and with some difficulty got them on his feet.

Strickland looked at the pointed riding boots and said, "No, McGrath, those won't do. Better try mine."

McGrath had larger feet than Strickland and the boots fit too tightly, but it was only a temporary thing. The rounder toes of the working boots would allow for better purchase on any footholds he might use.

He picked up a glove and started to put it on and thought better of it. Strickland tied the rope around McGrath's waist, then put a felt miner's hat on him and attached a candle spike and lit the candle it held.

The three men held up their candles, attempting to decide which wall afforded the best possibility for climbing. Having decided, they started McGrath up the wall and then pushed the raft away from it so that if he fell he would land in the water, not on the timbers.

The few hours of warmth and the jerky had done much to restore McGrath's strength, but the abuse his body had been subjected to over the past few days had taken a major toll on him and he felt it in the weakness of his muscles as he climbed. He concentrated all his energies on the task, and when he looked down he was surprised at how high he had climbed in a short time. When he reached the point where he could see the rim of the next level he realized he had also reached the end of his strength. His muscles were trembling from fatigue and he was afraid they would give out.

Watching him from below, holding their breath, Jackson and Strickland recognized what was happening. Strickland muttered, "He's not going to make it."

Jackson shouted, "McGrath, I know you can do this. Take a deep breath; you don't have much farther to go."

McGrath drew in a deep lungful of air and continued climbing. He reached the rim with his heart hammering inside his chest and his lungs unable to supply enough air for the exertion. He was able to pull himself to shoulder level and rest his arms on the rock floor, his boot toes resting on a slender outcropping, but he was simply unable to find the strength to pull his body over the rim.

"You can do it, McGrath," shouted Jackson. "I know you can."

McGrath made several attempts, but each time his muscles felt weaker. His leg muscles were trembling violently now.

Strickland shouted, "McGrath, we're all going to die in here because of you. It's just like a bloody Scotsman to give up when the bloody job is almost finished. Your father was a Scotsman and your grandfather was a Scotsman. Is that where you got it from? I'll bet they were just like you—couldn't finish a job."

Above them they heard a roar of agony, and McGrath vanished from view over the rim.

Jackson turned to Strickland. "Well done, Strickland."

"Sure, but now he'll probably leave us down here."

Despite their circumstances the two men managed a laugh.

Strickland's words, however, began to seem prophetic when nearly a half hour passed with no sign of McGrath. "He's left us," said Strickland.

"No," said Jackson, "I don't think so." Jackson didn't voice his fear, but he was afraid McGrath was dead.

They shivered with cold, shouting McGrath's name. Strickland shouted threats and insults, all to no avail and roughly two hours had passed when McGrath awoke and found himself lying on the rock floor. His candle was out. He was in complete darkness and at first he was confused, unable to remember where he was. Then it came to him, and he realized he must have passed out.

He could make out a very dim glow coming from the shaft and he crawled to the rim and peered over. Looking down he could dimly make out the shapes of the two men in the light of a single candle. He tried to think of something humorous to say, but his mind wasn't working well enough. All he could manage was, "What time is it?"

The two men gave a lurch of surprise. "McGrath, where have you been?" demanded Strickland. "We're freezing to death down here."

"Took a nap."

"Are you going to leave us down here?"

Remembering Strickland's insults, McGrath said, "Just so."

Strickland acted worried, but Jackson said, "McGrath, make two turns around a timber with the rope. Make sure the timber is solid and hold onto the end of the rope. All you have to do is pull out the slack as Strickland climbs. And hold tight if he slips off."

With another rope wrapped around his waist, Strickland started the climb. McGrath took out the slack as he moved up the wall. Because of his hand and the fact that his fingers were numb from being cold, Strickland slipped off the wall several times, but he merely hung there until he was able to regain a grip. And without major incident he was soon being helped over the rim by McGrath.

Next they pulled up their supplies, and afterward they were able to bring Jackson up to that level. All three men were wearing wet clothing, and they immediately found some timber and started a fire, the smoke being drawn up the shaft.

When their clothes were fully dried and their bodies warmed up Jackson and Strickland sat by the fire talking, while McGrath lay against the rib and slept.

"I know where we are," said Strickland, "and if we can get to where we need to go, we might be able to figure out how to get out of here. For right now, I think McGrath has the right idea. It feels like it's nighttime outside. I'm going to get some sleep."

"Me too," said Jackson. "My whole body aches."

Hours later when Jackson awoke, Strickland was already awake. McGrath was still sleeping, but he soon stirred, awakened by their talking.

"How're you feeling?" Jackson asked him.

"Empty as a post hole. Know any place around here where I can get a good beefsteak?" The weakness in his voice worried Jackson.

They gathered their equipment, helped McGrath to his feet, and

Strickland led the way. Ten minutes of walking brought them to another vertical shaft, which marked the end of the level they were in. High up on the opposite side of the shaft, was the opening to another level.

Strickland said, "Up there's where we need to be." He held up his candle and the light showed a smooth wall. He said, "That level doesn't continue on this side and there's no way a man can climb that wall. But we've got to get up there."

"How?" said Jackson.

"We make ourselves a ladder."

"A ladder?" said Jackson skeptically. "It's got to be twenty-five feet."

"More like thirty," said Strickland. "One thing we're not lacking in this mine is timbers and we've got plenty of rope. We'll lash the timbers together."

"And how will we get it up there? It'll be too long and heavy for us to lift."

Strickland contemplated this for a few moments and then sat down, leaning back against the rib. "There's got to be a way."

McGrath was sitting against the opposite rib. Holding his candle he began using a small, jagged rock to draw lines in the dust on the floor. At length he said, "First we build a bridge across the shaft. It will have to be a strong one. Then we build our ladder upward from the bridge."

"Yes," said Strickland after a few moments of contemplation. "Yes. It'll work."

Removing timbers was a dangerous thing—they were there for a reason. And they were solidly set, making the process difficult as well. The men were careful not to remove more than two or three timbers in a row before they skipped twenty feet or so and removed some more. But soon they had their bridge built across the shaft.

Because of the weight of each timber, a ladder with two legs would have been unmanageably heavy, so the three men devised a system of ropes with loops in them which attached to the segmented pole they were creating. Lashing the timbers together, each timber overlapping the last, they lengthened the ladder a timber at a time, lifting it from the bottom and allowing the top end to simply slide up the wall. By the time it was long enough it was almost too heavy for the three of them together to lift.

When it was finally finished, McGrath collapsed and had to be helped back across the bridge to where they had left their supplies.

Strickland said, "I can do this one," and immediately began to climb.

Jackson stood at the bottom of the ladder, steadying it, and soon Strickland was at the top, carrying a rope with him as always. He tossed one end down and Jackson secured it around McGrath's torso. In this way Strickland helped lift McGrath as he climbed.

With McGrath at the top, the rope was thrown back down and Jackson sent up the supplies and then followed, with both McGrath and Strickland holding the rope above.

At the top Jackson said, "I think it's time for another rest."

They built a fire and Strickland said, "There's a spring not far from here. I'll take the canteen and fill it." He emptied one of the canvas sacks they were carrying their equipment in and threw it over his shoulder.

Jackson said, "What's that for?"

Strickland said, "I'll be back shortly."

When he was gone Jackson said to McGrath, "Well at least we're warm and dry." He waited for an answer but none came. McGrath was asleep. Jackson mumbled to himself, "Don't die on me McGrath."

Jackson had no idea how long he had slept, but when he woke, Strickland had not returned. McGrath was still asleep and had not moved. The timber they had started on fire had burned through in the center and the fire was almost out, so Jackson slid one of the halves over and blew on the ashes until it began burning again. He was worried now. Had Strickland abandoned them? Why would he? If he knew of a way out, there would be no reason for him to take it himself and leave them in the mine.

He shouted Strickland's name and it echoed hollowly in the tunnel—or level as Strickland insisted on it being called. The miner had informed them that a tunnel was open to the outside on both ends. What they were in now was called a level. And a tunnel that was open to the outside on only one end was called an adit.

Jackson shouted again but there was no answer. He wasn't sure whether to go searching for Strickland or to wait for the Cornishman to return. He sat down again, staring at the fire for a while, wondering how Bonnie and Ruth were doing. They would be worried. Not wanting to worry them, he had not told them where he was going or why. He had sworn Strickland to secrecy as well, and now the three of them were trapped in here and no one friendly to them knew where they were.

Presently he heard a sound. He looked and saw the glow of a candle approaching. It was Strickland and he was carrying some items and grinning broadly. "It's Christmas time in the mine," he said. "I'm no Greek, but I come bearing all sorts of gifts." He set the articles down and began proudly showing them to Jackson.

"This is a miner's lunch pail," he said handing the pail to Jackson.

Jackson opened it and found that it contained three compartments. It was wet inside and out. "Some miner left it inside," said Strickland. "It had some scraps of moldy food in it and I had to scrub it out. Take that bottom part out and hold it over the fire and heat up what's inside."

"What is inside?" asked Jackson.

"Mush."

"Mush?" said Jackson in complete bewilderment.

"Corn mush. I ground it myself."

"Where did you get corn?"

At this, Strickland produced a bulging flour sack and said, "We've plenty of corn, my friend. We may get tired of it, but we won't go hungry. It's cracked corn," he explained, "It's the best food for the mules. That's why I wanted to get us up to this level. Not far from here is a place where we stored some of our supplies. There's mule food—hay and cracked corn, cribbing block, candles, timbers, rope, cable . . ."

"Why was it just left in here?" asked Jackson.

"They're planning to reopen the mine soon. That's the only reason I've stayed around these parts." He handed Jackson a spoon and said, "Better stir the mush."

Jackson stirred the mush, tasted it, and said, "McGrath, wake up, dinner's ready."

McGrath stirred, opened his eyes, and slowly, weakly, pushed himself to a seated position. "Did you say something?" he asked.

"Dinner time," said Jackson.

McGrath rubbed his eyes, "That would be nice." But when Jackson handed him the tray with the hot, steaming mush McGrath accepted it without question and wolfed it down. "Thank you," he said with genuine feeling as he handed it back to Jackson.

"Thank Strickland, not me," said Jackson.

Meanwhile, Strickland had searched until he had found a rock that was somewhat concave and another that was rounded and he was now grinding more of the cracked corn. This he poured into the little pan and added some water from the canteen and Jackson heated it. They continued this process until each man had eaten several bowls-full of mush and then they leaned back contentedly and relaxed.

Strickland said to McGrath, "Is what I heard about you true?"

"What did you hear?"

"That you are a gunfighter."

"Not really."

"But you killed that one cove, what was his name? Evan something."

"Santry," offered Frank Jackson. "And Guy Mustin. I've been curious about that too. You must be pretty fast, McGrath."

McGrath smiled. "There's a trick to it. I beat them both to the draw because I knew right when they were going to go for their guns and I started my pull just a little before they did."

"How could you know when they would draw?" asked Jackson.

"I insulted them. Men like Mustin and Santry are proud and hotheaded. You insult them and they grab iron. It's how they react."

Jackson merely smiled and shook his head.

Strickland said, "Isn't that just like a bloody Scotsman?" But he was smiling.

McGrath slept again for a couple of hours, awoke, and ate again and Jackson was pleased with the change he observed in the young man. Afterward, Strickland took the pan and washed it in a trickle of water that flowed nearby out of a crack in the rock.

When he returned he said, "Not far from here there's a gallery."

"What's a gallery?" asked Jackson.

"A natural hole inside the mountain. It's like a cave except with no opening. They come in all different sizes. This one is huge. On one of the levels we were working, we mined into it. If we can get to that level we can get out of this place."

"How high up is that level?"

"About a hundred feet. And there is no way for a man to climb it. The rock is too smooth. I think it was a giant bubble inside the mountain at one time, so it's rounded. It slopes inward as it goes up."

"Then how do you propose we get up there?"

"We build a tower."

"A hundred-foot tower? How is that possible?" asked McGrath. "We were barely able to manage a thirty-foot one."

"This one will be different. And we have different materials now—much better materials."

They stood in front of the supply cache and walked between the haulage tracks that ran down the center of the narrow aisle that had been left between the piles of supplies on either side. This went on for several-hundred feet. At the end of the adit, several large canvas bags had been hung from the ceiling or, as Strickland called it, the back, of the mine. This, he explained was the cracked corn for the feeding of the mules. It was hung there to keep rats from getting to it. Beneath the sacks was a flat car.

"That'll keep us alive for a good long time," Strickland said, pointing to the hanging sacks of corn. Nearby there were neatly stacked piles of crib blocks; large rectangular blocks of wood; rolls of rope and steel cable; an assortment of tools; and kegs of spikes, nails, ring bolts, clamps, and sundry other kinds of mining hardware.

From the supply cache, Strickland led them to the gallery. It was an impressive chamber nearly a hundred feet across at the base and so high that their candles failed to illuminate the top. Nor, unfortunately, were they able to see the level they would be striving to attain.

Strickland said, "We'll have to build a big fire so we can see what we're doing, because we have to build the base of our tower at exactly the right spot or the top won't line up with the opening of the next level." They built the fire, and McGrath announced that he was hungry.

"Me too," said Jackson, "Mush doesn't last very long in the stomach."

They went back to their old fire and gathered up all their supplies. McGrath made a point of picking up the stones Strickland had been using to grind the cracked corn. Back at the chamber he said, "I can make my own mush." And Jackson was immensely pleased at the vitality he heard in the voice.

McGrath ate and slept as Jackson and Strickland planned. Holding fire brands aloft, they located the opening to the next level and marked a corresponding spot on the floor of the chamber. They then went to the supply cache and began loading materials onto the flat car, afterward pushing the car down to the adit which led to the chamber. There were no tracks in this adit so the supplies had to be hand-carried or dragged the rest of the way to the chamber, which was, fortunately, only a short distance.

They worked for several hours, during which time McGrath had awakened, cooked and eaten more mush, and then joined them. Presently they went back to the fire and rested and planned some more. They were all tired and they agreed to treat this point as if it were night time. They would rest well and start on their tower in an estimated eight hours. For a time, they sat looking at the fire and casually talking. They spoke of home and family, or at least Strickland and Jackson did; McGrath had no home, and he had no family. Jackson spoke of his children, his grandchildren, and his wife, who was dead. Strickland told them of his life in Cornwall and then he said, "I have a wife there."

Jackson turned to face Strickland, not saying anything.

"Haven't seen her in nearly two years. When the tin mines played out over there and I got laid off, I came across with some other Cornishmen and found work here in the Crazy Horse. Sally and I had a plan. I was to work hard and save. No gambling, no drinking. I would save as much as I could and send money back home for her to come across. And we were going to start our family here in America."

"You don't have any children?" asked McGrath.

"No, I sailed the day after we were married. My Sally, she's such a sweet girl. She writes me faithfully. I don't know when I'll see her again now that the mine's closed. I've been trying to get work in one of the other mines, but they don't want me because of this hand." He held up his three fingered hand. "I don't know what to do. I don't have the money to go back home, nor can I bring Sally over."

"I'll make you a deal," said Jackson. "You get us out of this hole, and I'll give you the money to bring your wife over. And you can come to work with McGrath and me. We'll teach you the cattle business."

Strickland sprang to his feet and said, "Well, then gentlemen. It's time for us to get to work."

Jackson laughed and said, "Not me. I'm going to get some sleep. You'd both better do the same. We've got a giant-sized piece of work ahead of us."

The weather had been hot, but it had rained all night before the day of Vince Hamm's trial. It was raining still, and with the windows of the courtroom open, the temperature inside was comfortable.

The pending trial had attracted a good deal of attention and the room was packed. After the witnesses—all Spearhead men—had testified, each man telling the same story, most people in the room, even those who believed in Vince Hamm's innocence, already had him convicted and hanged. It looked that cut and dried.

Hamm's attorney, who was a local man and well liked, was a young lawyer named Beveridge. The jury was composed of local men, and Beveridge had fought and won the battle to exempt Spearhead riders from service thereon.

Redmond, the prosecuting attorney, was from out of town. He was a tall, rotund, red-faced man. Expensively dressed and patently self-assured, he exhibited a much more imposing presence than his opponent. Pompous by nature, he was made more pompous by his confidence in what promised to be an easy victory.

Redmond had easily established that Vince Hamm and Les Perkins had been enemies in the past and that Hamm, on one occasion, while intoxicated, had threatened to kill the rancher.

Beveridge had battled nobly to defend his client, but thus far had had very little to fight with, aside from statements of good character by local people who knew Hamm. But character references would not overbalance the several eyewitness accounts that the prosecution had provided—or rather had been provided to him by Spearhead. Beveridge was a worried man, and Vince Hamm was mentally preparing his last will and testament.

Tom Lee Maryann, who had made it a point to stay sober for this occasion, was in the back and had been observing the proceedings.

Now he came forward and passed a note to Beveridge, who read it and immediately turned around to face Tom Lee. Tom Lee said nothing, and after a moment's deliberation Beveridge nodded.

"Either of you two have any more witnesses?" asked the circuit judge.

Redmond said, "No, Your Honor.

Beveridge hesitated for a moment, then said, "I do, Your Honor."

Looking old and frail, Tom Lee sat in the witness chair and was instructed to place his hand on the Bible and state his name. At this, he seemed to hesitate. He sat with his trembling right hand raised, not speaking, until finally the judge said, "Your name, Sir, your name."

Finally, Tom Lee spoke, "Folks call me Tom Lee Maryann."

Redmond had been reading a note that had been passed to him by Marshall Croft. He stuffed the note in his pocket and, rising to his feet, said, "Your Honor, I object to this witness. He is . . ."

"Overruled. Sit down, Counselor."

Tom Lee was sworn in, and Beveridge stood up. Addressing Tom Lee he said, "A few minutes ago you gave me a note indicating you had knowledge about the events of the night of April twelfth of this year. Knowledge that could help prove my client's innocence. Is that true?"

"Yes, Sir."

"Can you tell us what that information is?"

"Yes. I sometimes go for walks in the evening and on that particular evening . . ."

Beveridge interrupted, "April twelfth of this year in the evening, correct?"

"Yes."

"Continue."

"I went for a walk that evening to where I often go; up into the trees north of town. I saw a horse in the trees where he couldn't be seen from any other place. He was saddled and standing tied to a tree. I saw the brand."

"And what was the brand?"

"It was Lazy Nine. I know whose brand that is."

"And whose brand is it?"

"It's the brand of Mr. Francisco Soto, who owns the livery stable."

Not having had the opportunity to confer with this witness beforehand, Beveridge was at a disadvantage. At this point all he could do was ask the question, "Was there anything else?"

"Yes. The horse had been there for several hours, I could tell."

"How could you tell that, Mr. Maryann?"

"By the droppings on the ground, but also by something else."

"And what was that something else?"

"There was a bird's nest in the tree directly above the horse, and a large amount of bird droppings had fallen on the saddle."

"And was there anything else significant?"

"About the horse?"

"Your Honor, I object," exclaimed Redmond. "The witness appears to be leading the examiner."

"Sustained. You know what to do, Mr. Beveridge."

"Yes, Your Honor. So, Mr. Maryann, what other unusual thing or things did you observe about the horse?"

"Well, right then, nothing, but later that horse was claimed to be the one Vince Hamm was riding when he was supposed to have shot Les Perkins. You know that I sometimes help out in the livery stable. I was there that night when the sheriff brought the horse in. The pile of bird droppings was still in the saddle and had not been disturbed. No one, not even a child, could have ridden that horse without disturbing it."

Beveridge looked at the judge to make sure the judge was paying full attention. He was.

Beveridge said, "Did you make any other observations?"

"No, Sir."

"That's all I have for this witness, Your Honor."

"Mr. Redmond?" the circuit judge said.

"Yes, Your Honor, I do have some questions." He stood up and walked over to the witness box, exuding confidence. "Mr. Maryann, I'm sorry you had such a difficult time understanding what was wanted when you were asked to state your name. If any of the questions I ask you cause too much mental strain, please so indicate and I will make every attempt to simplify them for you."

A murmur of indignation arose from the crowd. The judge raised his gavel, but silence was restored before he had to bring it down.

Tom Lee said in all apparent sincerity, "Thank you, Sir. You're very kind."

"Mr. Maryann, this horse you saw, can you tell us where it came from?"

"No, Sir."

"Can you tell us who put it there?"

"No, Sir."

Redmond raised bushy eyebrows and shook an admonitory finger at Tom Lee. "Sir, a man's life is at stake here. You volunteered to help; now you must do so. Will you tell us who tied that horse to that tree?"

"No, I . . ."

Redmond interrupted, "So you refuse to tell us?"

"I don't refuse, Sir. I just . . ."

"Do you drink, Mr. Maryann?" interrupted Redmond again.

"Yes, Sir."

"When was the last time you drank?"

"I had some water before I came over here today."

General laughter ensued. This time the judge did bring down his gavel and shouted, "Order!"

Redmond waited for silence to return. "As I promised you, Mr. Maryann, I will attempt to make my questions simple and understandable. When was the last time you drank liquor?" He emphasized the last word, pronouncing each syllable slowly.

"Yesterday, Sir."

"And did you get drunk?"

"Yes I did."

"Do you drink every day?"

"Yes I do."

"Do you get drunk every day?"

"Yes I do."

"Will you hold out your hands?"

"Objection, Your Honor," said Beveridge.

"What's your point, Mr. Redmond?" said the circuit judge.

"I am merely trying to establish what is a well-known fact in this community: that Mr. Maryann is a drunkard, and therefore his testimony is not to be taken seriously. His hands are trembling at this moment from the lack of his daily liquor. He is to be viewed as an unreliable witness."

The judge turned to Tom Lee. "You said you haven't drunk liquor since yesterday."

"That's correct, Your Honor."

"Roughly at what time did you take your last drink?"

"Roughly eight o'clock, Your Honor."

"Eight in the morning, or eight at night?"

"At night, Your Honor."

"And you'll swear on the Bible that you haven't taken any liquor since then?"

"I will, Your Honor. And if you wish, I'll recite the Gettysburg Address to prove I'm sober."

"Just give us the first part."

"Four score and seven years ago . . .'"

Two paragraphs in, the judge stopped him and said, "That'll be enough, Mr. Maryann. I'll sustain the objection. The prosecution will refrain from asking any further questions about, or making any further allusions to, the witness's inebriate tendencies."

Even in acquiescence there was arrogance in the slight bow Redmond gave the judge. Turning back to Tom Lee he squared his shoulders, thrust out his jaw, and said, "Mr. Maryann. The only significant point in your testimony is whether or not you know who put that horse in that grove of trees."

"No, Sir, it isn't." countered Tom Lee. "The bird droppings are the significant point."

"Who put that horse there?" demanded Redmond, raising his voice.

"The bird droppings are what matter."

"Where did that horse come from, Sir?"

"The bird droppings, Sir. There was a pile of bird droppings on the saddle."

Beveridge seemed on the verge of objecting, but he shuttled his anxious glance back and forth between Tom Lee and the judge, and, seeing that Tom Lee seemed to be handling himself well, and the judge showed no indication of stopping the exchange, he relaxed and leaned back in his chair.

"Where did the horse come from Sir, where did it come from?" demanded Redmond, shouting.

Tom Lee was now standing, leaning toward Redmond. Redmond was leaning toward Tom Lee. They were shouting in each other's faces, and no one was stopping it.

"Where did the horse come from, Sir, where did it come from? I ask you, where did it come from?" shouted Redmond.

"The pile of bird excrement, Sir," shouted Tom Lee, "That's what matters."

"Where did it come from?" bellowed Redmond, his face bright red, shining with the lust of battle. "I insist you tell this court where it came from, Sir."

Tom Lee leaned back, suddenly very calm. "From birds, I assume, Sir. That's the only known source."

Pandemonium erupted in the courtroom. The tension that had built up was released now in hilarity. People laughed until they gasped, turning to each other, slapping each other on the back.

Struggling valiantly to maintain his own composure, the judge stood—without giving the bailiff a chance to say, "All rise,"—banged his gavel once, and said in a voice that was lost in the commotion, "Ten minute recess." He turned, walked out the door, and closed it behind him, and the sound of his laughter could be heard over the din he had left behind.

It was actually more than twenty minutes before the judge returned from the saloon where he had gone to have a drink. All rose, all were seated, and the trial was resumed. Tom Lee was seated again in the witness chair and the judge said, "Does anyone have any more questions for this witness?"

Beveridge said, "No, Your Honor."

Redmond shook his head sullenly. Tom Lee was dismissed. Both attorneys made eloquent final arguments, and the matter was turned over to the twelve male jurors. They did not deliberate long. The evidence Tom Lee had provided, they agreed, was sufficient to cast a reasonable doubt on Vince Hamm's guilt. It was also tacitly agreed, though not explicitly stated, that, while Tom Lee was a drunkard, he was their drunkard, and Redmond was an outsider and a pompous jackass to boot. They returned a verdict of not guilty.

Tom Lee was the man of the hour. He was given countless slaps on the back and numerous offers of a drink. The slaps on the back he accepted graciously, the drinks he declined. Tom Lee always drank alone.

CHAPTER 9

The tower progressed rapidly at first and increasingly more slowly the higher it grew. It was back-breaking work; loading the heavy crib blocks on the flat car, pushing the car to the chamber adit, and carrying the blocks the rest of the way into the chamber. But the hardest work of all was raising the heavy crib blocks to the top of the tower as it grew.

The men supported the tower laterally on four sides by using a system of cables which attached to the tower by ring bolts screwed into the wood, and to the rock wall of the gallery by means of spikes driven into crevices in the rock. They took turns doing different jobs, the most difficult and dangerous of them being that of standing on top of the tower and hauling up each individual block by rope, pulling it hand over hand and then setting it in place when it reached the top. This job, of course, became increasingly strenuous as the tower grew taller, and they were forced to create a pulley system so that the two men below could assist the top man in the raising of the blocks.

There was no night or day in the mine, and no way to reckon the passage of time—Jackson's watch had gotten full of water and quit working—so they rested when they felt like it and ate mush as often as they were hungry and pushed themselves as hard as they could when they worked. And the tower grew taller and the work harder and more dangerous.

But despite the difficulty of the endeavor and the frequent setbacks that were encountered, the moment finally arrived when McGrath, who happened to be taking his turn as top man, set the crib block in place that put the tower high enough for him to be able to reach the rim of the next level and pull himself up and over. Due to the poor illumination his two companions below were unable to witness the event, but he called down to them. "I'm up," and heard their joyous shouting below.

He dropped a rope down to make their ascent less perilous and soon the three men were together on the level they had worked so hard to achieve. They didn't bother hauling up their equipment; Strickland assured them they would no longer need it and, as he had promised, they were soon standing just outside the head frame of the Crazy Horse, smelling the fresh air and looking up at the stars.

They were on the opposite side of the mountain from where they had entered the mine and it took some time to walk down the rough haul road to town. When they reached the shack where Strickland lived, Jackson said, "Strickland, I don't know how the next few days will play out, so we'd better take care of some things right away. Tomorrow morning I'll go the bank and leave them my instructions for the money you'll need to get your bride over here. That way, no matter what happens to me, it'll be taken care of."

McGrath watched this scene. He could not see Strickland's face well in the darkness. The miner didn't say anything; he merely put a hand on Jackson's shoulder, then turned and walked to the door.

They had no way of determining what time it was, but as Jackson and McGrath walked toward Bonnie's house they saw that there were still plenty of comings and goings in the town and a lot of raucous noise coming from the saloons. Bonnie's restaurant, however, was closed, which told them it was past eight o'clock.

They knocked on the front door of Bonnie's house and soon she appeared in her nightdress and wrapper, holding a lamp. She threw the door open in the manner of a person who is anxiously expecting someone and immediately began to cry. Ruth appeared behind her, and the two women began making a great fuss over Jackson and McGrath, taking them immediately to the kitchen to feed them.

"We'll need to wash up first," protested Jackson.

"Wash up and then tell us where you've been," said Bonnie. "We've been worried sick. Your foreman came looking for you. He said you had left the ranch and hadn't been back in days. We talked to the sheriff and he checked around, but nobody knew where you were."

Between forkfuls Jackson attempted to answer their questions. McGrath spoke very little, intent on his eating. Bonnie sat next to Jackson and kept her hand on his arm. Ruth did not sit at the table, but stood against a wall, not saying much, her eyes mostly on McGrath.

When Jackson was finished with his narrative, Bonnie said, "Decker! I knew he had something to do with it. I saw him in town earlier. He was walking toward a saloon, acting like he was king of the world—the way he always does. He'll probably drink and gamble all night."

"You need to tell Sheriff Wardman what Decker did," said Ruth.

McGrath and Jackson exchanged a look. Jackson said, "What could he do? Decker would deny everything. Wardman can't fight Spearhead."

"This is our fight," murmured McGrath. He wolfed down his food and when he was finished, he excused himself and went upstairs. Later, when he did not return to the kitchen, Bonnie sent Ruth to look for him. Soon she came back and said, "He's gone and so are his gun belt and rifle."

McGrath knew which saloon Decker frequented and he went there. When he stepped inside, he spotted the man sitting at a deal table playing cards with three other men. There were no other Spearhead men in the saloon and McGrath found this interesting. Could it be that, thinking he had eliminated his enemies, Decker no longer felt the need to be constantly accompanied by a group of hired toughs?

It was late and the saloon would soon be closing for the night. Tom Lee was at the bar buying a bottle of whiskey, but aside from him, the bartender, and the men at Decker's table, the place was empty.

McGrath walked in, crossed the room, and without preamble, bashed Decker on the side of the head with the butt of his rifle, knocking him out of his chair. He stepped back, pointing the rifle at Decker but keeping his eye on the other men at the table. Decker rolled onto his back and grabbed for his gun.

"I wouldn't," said McGrath. "Touch that pistol and you're dead. Now pull it out and slide it across the floor."

Decker did as he was told.

"How'd it feel, Decker?" said McGrath. "You like bein' knocked on the head?"

Decker pulled himself to his feet, holding his hand to the side of his head, a look of astonishment on his face.

"That's right, Decker, it's me. I'm back from the dead to haunt you." He turned to the men at the table and said, "This is a private matter. Any objections?"

One of them said, "Not as long as you put your guns up."

McGrath set his guns on the bar and turned around to face Decker. Decker was the larger of the two, but McGrath had, in the past, pitted his strength against larger men and never found it wanting. More than that, however, he wanted this fight. He had carried with him for days a dark wrath every time he thought of Decker. He wanted this fight very badly.

Had Decker known the depth of McGrath's rage and the strength of his determination when he set his mind to a task, he would not have moved toward McGrath with the confidence he displayed at that moment. He closed in, swinging his fists and connecting only with air. And then, unexpectedly, he was struck in the mouth by a powerful blow that crushed his lips. Enraged, he bellowed and charged, still swinging. But McGrath wasn't there. He had sidestepped, and as Decker came past, McGrath struck him a solid blow on the side of the face. Unexpectedly, Decker spun, swinging a backhand that came around and hit McGrath on the cheekbone knocking him backward.

Seeing an opportunity, Decker moved in and swung a right and a left. McGrath ducked under the right but the left came up and hit him on the side of the mouth, splitting his lower lip. Decker moved in now, his arms outspread in an attempt to get McGrath in a bear hug. But McGrath was still crouched low and he shot upward, head-butting Decker under the shelf of his jaw.

Decker backed up, almost fell, and caught himself. McGrath too knew an opportunity when he saw one and he came in, swinging fast and hard, trying to end the fight before Decker could recover.

But Decker was far from being finished. He swung a right that connected solidly with McGrath's jaw. McGrath fell to the side and came up against the bar, turning quickly to meet Decker as the man came in. They grappled for a few moments, and then McGrath landed a hard right to Decker's nose and it spouted blood. Decker backed off, and for a time they both stood where they were, trying to catch their breath, too exhausted to continue.

It was then that McGrath noticed Frank Jackson standing near the door, watching.

"You all right, McGrath?" Jackson asked.

McGrath nodded.

Observing the fight, Jackson had been struck by the ferocity with which these men attacked each other. These were two men who hated each other. Neither of them would quit until he lacked the strength to lift his arms to strike another blow. They were resting now, but he knew they would be back at it soon.

He heard boots striking the boardwalk, and the jangle of spurs. He moved farther into the room to make way for the men who were entering, putting his hand on the pistol he had stuck in his waistband before leaving Bonnie's place. Two Spearhead riders came past him into the room, each holding a gun. One of them said, "We're backin' you, Decker."

Jackson was pulling his pistol when he felt a gun barrel jab him in the back, followed by the command, "Don't do it."

A hand reached around and took his pistol.

Decker had been leaning forward, supporting his hands on his thighs as his nose dripped blood. He straightened now and said, "Changes things." He walked over to where his pistol lay on the floor, bent down, and retrieved it. He cocked it and pointed it at McGrath.

From behind the bar there was the sound of a shotgun being cocked and Tom Lee, who had stood mostly unnoticed in the shadows near the back door, said, "Pull that trigger and in about half a second you'll be wonderin' where your head went."

Decker froze. From where Tom Lee stood, he had Decker covered as well as the men by the door.

"Captain Jackson," said Tom Lee, "move away."

Jackson understood his meaning and moved out of the line of fire, leaving the Spearhead men standing there in a clump.

"Tell your men to drop their guns," said Tom Lee to Decker.

Decker hesitated and Tom Lee said, "Decker, I've got nothin' to lose. I'm an old man and I'm a drunk. They'd be doin' me a favor by hangin' me. There's two barrels on this greener. You'll get the first one and your boys over there will split the second one among 'em."

Despite the frailty of his body, there was in Tom Lee's voice something that no one in this town had ever heard in him before: a commanding force and strength of purpose that bade him be obeyed. Decker lowered his gun to the floor and his men did the same. None of them wanted to be on the receiving end of a ten-gauge.

Tom Lee said, "Decker, take your men and ride back to

Spearhead."

Decker walked over to where his hat lay on the floor and picked it up. He walked toward the door but stopped and turned to face Tom Lee. "Next time I see you, I'll kill you."

"You probably will, Decker. You're that kind of coward."

When the Spearhead riders had gone, Jackson started across the room toward Tom Lee. Tom Lee raised the shotgun and said, "Stay back, Captain."

Jackson did not hesitate. As he came closer Tom Lee said, "I mean it, I'll blast you to kingdom come."

Jackson walked up to him, gently pushed the barrel of the shotgun aside, and said in a soft voice, "Ben."

Tom Lee dropped his eyes. He un-cocked the saloonkeeper's shotgun, set it on the bar, and turned away.

"Wait," said Jackson.

"No, Captain. Leave me alone. Don't follow me." And taking his bottle of whiskey from the counter, Tom Lee left through the back door.

Jackson stood gazing at the closed door for a good thirty seconds. Finally he turned to McGrath and looked at him for a moment. "Feel better now?"

"Uh huh."

"That was pretty stupid."

"But it felt good."

Vince Hamm was free, Jeremiah was dead, and McGrath had disappeared. Hamm wandered around town like a lost soul, unable to plan even for his immediate future. He couldn't go back to his ranch; Spearhead controlled the whole of it, and there was no point in ending up like Jeremiah.

He stopped in at the bank and took out a little money. In view of the fact that McGrath had vanished, Hamm was glad he hadn't given the young man authorization to withdraw money from his account, though there had not been much money there. A similar amount had been hidden in Hamm's office at the ranch house. Hamm had told McGrath where to find it and only McGrath knew what had become of it—and McGrath had disappeared.

Hamm stopped at the post office and found that it had been some time since McGrath had picked up Flying V's mail. There was a letter addressed to the Flying V from a man named Dixon. Hamm opened it and found that it was meant for McGrath.

Dear Mr. McGrath,
As you told us to expect, someone representing Flying V came for the herd you left in our keeping. Thank you for the money you gave us. My boy only watched your herd for less than a month. We feel we owe you some money back. Please write to let us know what you want us to do.
Sincerely,
Arnold Dixon

Vince Hamm sat down on the boardwalk, absorbing this information. He absently folded the letter and put it in his pocket, and it came to him that he had been cleaned out. This explained why McGrath had not come to visit him in jail after that first time. It also explained why McGrath had disappeared. He had stolen the herd, driven it far away, and arranged for someone, probably cattle buyers, to go take possession of it.

He sat there feeling like a fool. He had placed his trust—his ranch; everything he owned—in the hands of a man he had known for a little over a week. And this was the result. He felt betrayed. He felt old. He felt humiliated. He felt no anger, except at himself. But it would come, he knew. It would come.

Hamm was a proud man. He resolved to tell no one of McGrath's perfidy—he was too embarrassed. He would simply let people believe the totality of the blame lay with Spearhead. But, how he would make his living for the remainder of his life, he did not know. All he knew was ranching. He could still work, but could a man his age get hired on as a cowboy? And, if so, how much longer could he continue doing that brutal work? And when he was no longer able, then what? He looked at his future and he was afraid. And he felt the anger start to build.

The next day, quite by accident, he saw Colin McGrath walk into Bonnie's Restaurant.

"I'm worried about Tom Lee," said Ruth to Bonnie. It was late afternoon and they hadn't seen the man for two days. "I think I'll go check on him."

"Good idea."

The voice that came back to Ruth when she knocked on Tom Lee's door was clearly not the voice of a healthy man. "Are you all right, Tom Lee?" she queried.

"Fine."

Unconvinced, Ruth said, "Can I come in?"

There was a long silence and then she heard Tom Lee say, "Not proper."

"No it isn't, but can I come in?"

Another long silence. "Alright."

He was lying on his cot, soaked in sweat. His face was pale, his features pinched.

"Tom Lee," she asked, "how long's it been since you ate?"

"Not sure."

"How long have you been sick?"

"Couple days."

"I'll bring you some food." She left and returned shortly with a plate of food covered with a cloth. "Eat this, Tom Lee."

He sat up and reached for the plate, but his hands were trembling so badly that she said, "Let me do it."

She fed him a few forkfuls and he promptly threw them up. "Can't eat right now," he said as she wiped up his mess. "Leave the food. I'll eat it later."

She knew what the problem was but was not sure how to approach it. "Sometimes a drink can help the appetite." She finally said.

His mouth worked. He licked his lips. "Sometimes it does."

She smiled. "Let's try it and see. I'll be back."

Three doors down from the restaurant was a saloon. She walked to its back door and knocked loudly, and she was not sure if she had been heard over the noise within. She knocked again and the swamper stuck his head out.

She knew him. "Grady," she said, "How much is a bottle of whiskey?"

Acting a little surprised, Grady asked, "What kind of whiskey?"

"The kind Tom Lee drinks."

"Oh," he said with a knowing nod, "I was wonderin'. . . ."

"Will you bring it?" she interrupted.

He brought it and she paid him for it and took it back over to Tom Lee's shack.

There was no furniture in Tom Lee's single room except for his cot and an upturned crate which served as a table. She set the bottle on it and said, "I'll be checking on you if it's alright."

He shook his head. "I'll probably feel better by tomorrow."

"No, Tom Lee, I will bring food every day and you will eat it. If you don't, eat you'll die."

"Wouldn't mind that, Ma'am," he murmured, "Wouldn't mind it much at all."

McGrath was unspeakably relieved when he learned that while he had been trapped in the mine, Vince Hamm's trial had been held and the rancher had been exonerated. He searched for Hamm, but, though he talked to numerous people who had recently seen him, he was unable to find him. Realizing it had been too long since he had checked on the horse herd, he rode out with that purpose, wishing he had been able to locate Hamm so they could do this together.

The horses were where he had left them, and it was time to move them again. He didn't look forward to it, because every time he moved them, in each new canyon he took them to, he had to build another brush fence—a dirty and disagreeable task. The sun was going down and it was too late to start a round up, so he set about making camp for the night. He was bent over his fire, frying bacon, when a voice came from behind.

"Make one move, you snake, and I'll perforate you."

Recognizing the voice, thinking the threat was in fun, McGrath turned around, a smile beginning. But there was no smile on the face of Vince Hamm. And he was pointing a rifle.

"Seen you in town, McGrath. I hid out and waited for you to leave and follered you here. I'm a pretty good Injun when I try; been doin' it since before your ma and pa was ever born. Drop your gun and keep in mind this Winchester is loaded."

Puzzled, McGrath put his pistol on the ground and said, "What's eatin' you, Boss? I sure don't remember steppin' on your corn."

"Back up, you miserable gut-wagon buzzard."

McGrath backed up and Hamm picked up his pistol, shoving it in his belt. He motioned with his head toward the grazing herd of horses. "Nice herd you've got there, McGrath. Look a lot like some horses I used to own."

"Is that the problem? Are you thinkin' I . . ."

"Shut up. I ain't interested in listenin' to any of your lies."

"Then what do you want?"

"To watch you waller in the dirt with a gut full of lead would be my first choice. Wish't my son was here. Simon'd turn you so inside out you'd get sunburned liver."

McGrath pointed to the fire. "Bacon's burnin'."

"Stay where you're at." Hamm reached down and removed the pan from the fire. He said, "I follered you here and now I'll get my horses back. But you stole my cows, and I want the money you got paid for 'em."

"There is no money. I didn't sell 'em." McGrath could have said much more. He could have told the rancher about the events of the perilous trail drive and the Farmer whose boy was tending the herd—all for the purpose of salvaging at least a part of Flying V's livestock so that Hamm would have something left when he got out of jail—but he was too offended by Hamm's accusations to permit himself to give the man any explanations.

"Didn't sell 'em, 'eh?" said Hamm. "I believe that. I sure do." He pulled a folded envelope out of a pocket and tossed it to McGrath, who opened it, struck a match, and read it. It was the letter from Farmer Dixon. McGrath was puzzled. The letter said that someone representing Flying V had taken the herd. How was that possible? Completely bewildered he asked, "When did this come?"

"Ain't fun to be found out, is it?"

Then it came to McGrath. The only other person who knew about the herd and where it was being held was Hamm's son, Simon. McGrath had written to him, telling him everything. He would be the only person who would show up personally—or send someone else—claiming to be a representative of Flying V or of McGrath, and drive the herd away—and this while his father was in jail, awaiting trial for the charge of murder.

Suddenly, McGrath felt a great pity for Vince Hamm. The betrayal the old man felt in believing McGrath had deceived him was nothing compared to what it would be if he knew the real truth. So, McGrath set the letter on the ground and was silent.

Hamm nodded. "Not much you can say, is there? I hate a liar, McGrath, and I hate a thief. Just lookin' at you gags me." He picked a piece of bacon out of the pan, blew on it, and put it in his mouth. Chewing, he said, "I want the money."

Remembering the reward money he had been paid for the killing of Evan Santry, McGrath said, "Alright. It's in the bank."

"Knew you'd cave. Folded like a wet feed sack. Ain't no straw at all in your plaster. In my day a man like you wouldn't have even lasted to be growed up. And if he did, we would've hung 'im."

It was fully dark now and the small fire gave off only a dim light. McGrath reached around behind him and picked up a rock. Hamm was hungry, he could tell. When the rancher reached for another piece of bacon, McGrath threw the rock and launched himself across the space between them. The rock hit Hamm on the side of the head, and an instant later, McGrath struck him, knocking him into the dirt. Within two seconds McGrath had the rifle and the pistol and was standing over Hamm.

He could sense Hamm's fear, and he felt only pity for the man. He said, "I'm leavin' now, Vince. You can finish the bacon. I'll leave your rifle with the banker. I'll deposit two-thousand dollars in your account and we'll be even. Agreed?"

There was a grunt of assent. Hamm was in no position to argue.

McGrath said, "The horses need to be moved. This canyon is grazed out." He turned to walk away, then turned back and said, "The horse I'm ridin' belongs to you, Vince. I'll get it back to you as soon as I can get another one. I took the money from your hidin' place in the office and paid Jeremiah with it. After I paid off a few of Flying V's accounts in town, there wasn't much left. You see, they figured you were going to hang and they wanted their money."

McGrath didn't mention the fact that there had not been enough money left over to even pay his wage. He had worked for nothing. He saddled his horse and rode away; hungry, but unutterably relieved to be released from the responsibility of being the foreman of the Flying V ranch.

It was early in the morning; in fact it was still dark, when Frank Jackson rode out to the Double Circle, arriving there at first light. There was no one around and every building had been burned to the ground. A superannuated milk cow grazed placidly in the pasture, but otherwise there was no life to be seen. Hurriedly Jackson made a circuit of the area and was relieved to find no bodies or fresh graves. At least there was hope that his men were safe, but now what?

From the corner of his eye he saw a flash of light, the sun reflecting off something shiny. It was repeated again and again as he watched it. Someone was signaling him from up on Silent Mountain. Was it his crew, or was it a trap? Jackson thought about this for a few moments and decided it was probably his crew. He would ride up there, stay out in the open, and find out.

When he had ridden far enough in the direction of the flash to make his intention known, it stopped. He kept alert, constantly watching his back trail and the surrounding area. He saw no one and no one's dust. As he approached the bluffs and the land began to rise, he reined in. This was as far as he would go. Friend or foe they would have to send someone out to greet him before he would ride into those rocks.

He waited and soon a man came riding out of a gap in the wall of rock. As he approached, Jackson recognized his foreman, Jerome. As Jerome drew near, Jackson spurred to meet him and said, "Is everyone alright?"

"Sure, Boss."

"How many do we have?"

"Eight. Allen and Colby sloped."

"How've you boys been living?"

"We were ready. When you disappeared, we figured they'd come. We cached food and supplies over in a canyon." He pointed back toward the bluffs. "Blankets, firewood, a few things like that, plenty of ammunition. We got all the ranch papers too. We figured they'd burn the buildings."

"Good thinking," said Jackson, vastly relieved to know that the ranch's records and legal documents had not been destroyed.

Jerome continued, "We posted lookouts and then we waited. We figured they'd come at night and they did—about twenty-five of 'em. When we knew they were comin', we sloped on out of there and here we sit, waitin' for you, Boss."

Jerome took Jackson along a twisting trail to where the rest of the men were hidden. They'd picked a good place. There was plenty of shelter from the elements, and it was highly defensible. With enough ammunition, five or six men could hold off a small army.

Jerome had a pair of field glasses hanging around his neck. Recognizing them as his own, Jackson asked for them and, following a well-used trail, the two men climbed to the top of the bluff, where they spent the next few hours taking turns with the field glasses. It was mid-morning when they saw dust rising up from the vicinity of Spearhead headquarters. The dust moved eastward and then separated into two sources. Decker had divided his men into two groups.

Jackson turned to Jerome and said, "How long have they been hunting you?"

"Three days."

"Have you been watching them?"

"Yeah. We snuck up on 'em night before last. Didn't get too close, but we saw where they was camped. We went back last night and found 'em camped in the same place."

"Why would they camp two nights in a row in the same place?"

"Appears they go out for a couple of days at a time. They have a lot of supplies cached in a bowl. There's a little spring there. They use that as their base."

"Well then, let's go pay them a visit tonight."

It was late in the day when Jerome, who was taking a turn with the field glasses, said, "Someone followin' your tracks."

"Let me see." Jackson watched the rider for a few moments and recognized him as Colin McGrath. They rode out to meet McGrath and Frank greeted him warmly. Grinning, he said, "Come on back to camp, Colin. We'll feed you some corn mush."

"Keep talkin' like that and I'll go back to work for Spearhead."

With nothing to do but wait for night to come, the day dragged slowly for the crew of the Double Circle. Jackson and Jerome and McGrath took turns keeping watch with the field glasses until, finally, in the deepening dusk, Jackson said to the men, "Let's go."

The horses had already been saddled and now the men mounted and Jerome led the way, with Jackson and McGrath riding on either side of him. They rode slowly, knowing that though their dust could not be seen in the dark it could be smelled. And the sound of fast-moving horses could be heard from far off. There was no hurry. . . they had all night.

This was not new to Jackson. He had been an officer in the United States Army and had fought in a war. He knew how to lead men into battle. It was a good thing he did, because on this night this half of the Spearhead crew had chosen not stay in the bowl, but only to eat supper there.

In a wide, steep-sided canyon, Jackson raised his hand and halted the group. He said urgently to Jerome, "Spread the men around higher up on the slopes so they won't shoot each other. Tell them to ready their weapons—and make sure they do it quietly."

McGrath rode on ahead and immediately came back. "I smell dust."

When Jackson's order was accomplished, Jerome said, "What's up, Boss? I don't hear anything."

"Just a feeling. McGrath thinks so too."

Less than two minutes later the Spearhead riders rode into the canyon.

When Jackson yelled, "Fire," the Double Circle riders did so from all sides, cutting through the shocked Spearhead crew.

McGrath saw a group of Spearhead men break off from the rest and move in his direction. He spurred his horse hard, firing his pistol at dim shapes as they came toward him. A gun discharged almost in his face, nearly deafening him with the concussion. He ran into the man and slashed downward with his pistol, feeling it connect solidly.

All around men were shouting and firing. Someone shouted, "I'm hit, Sid, I'm hit."

"Over here," another man shouted.

Now there was no way to know who was enemy and who was friend, and the firing became sporadic. McGrath reined his horse around and raced back toward the ravine that led into the canyon. Near the entrance someone said, "Who's that? Who's that?" To answer would be foolish in case it was a Spearhead rider. Not to answer was certain to bring gun fire in his direction.

Ducking low on his horse, he said, "Who are you?"

The man recognized his voice. "McGrath?"

"Yes."

"Alright, alright."

It was pretty certain that nobody else had gotten past this point so

McGrath told the man, "Keep this end bottled up."

Most of the firing had died down now and he rode back to the opposite end of the canyon through a short defile that opened into the bowl where the Spearhead riders had been spending their nights. In this light, shadows took on the shape and form of a man, and if one stared at a shadow long enough it seemed to move.

He stopped near the opening to the bowl and listened and heard faint hoof beats. He went back to the canyon where, in the moonlight, he could see men and horses milling around. On the ground there were the shapes of several downed men and two horses. He identified Frank Jackson's high shape on his horse and rode over to him.

"We got six of them," volunteered Jackson. "They got one of ours and two others are wounded."

"Decker?"

"Not with them. Maybe he got away."

"Maybe," said McGrath. "Some of them did." Then he asked, "Who'd they kill?"

"Newton."

"How bad are the wounded?"

"Blaine is pretty bad. Herschel's is nothing serious."

Jerome rode up and joined them and Jackson said, "McGrath thinks some of them made it out. Where do you think they'll go?"

"Back to Spearhead."

"That's what I'm thinking, too," said Jackson. "But they'll have to go the long way around. If we ride back down the ravine we can cut them off."

Leaving a man to take care of the two wounded Double Circle Riders, they called for the able-bodied to mount up and follow. Once they were out in the open they talked as they rode.

Jerome said, "There's three ways they can get back to Spearhead. Two of 'em involve some pretty hard ridin'. If any of 'em are wounded, they probably won't pick either of those trails."

"You're thinking of the river crossing," said McGrath.

"That's right."

"Then, let's go," said Jackson.

They made it there a good twenty minutes before the Spearhead riders did and waited for them to get out to the middle of the river before Jackson called to them to halt and throw down their guns.

The Spearhead men began firing and the Double Circle men fired back. The water was stirrup deep, and the horses were unable to move quickly. At the outset two more Spearhead riders fell. There were only two left now and they threw down their weapons and raised their arms.

McGrath and another rider rode out into the river and made sure the two had no weapons. The prisoners and the dead men were brought to the shore and their faces scrutinized by match light, the captors hoping one of them would be Decker. None of them was. One of the prisoners and one of the dead men had been wounded in the fight in the canyon.

Jerome said to Jackson, "We're pretty close to Spearhead now. If Decker and his crew are nearby, they'll have heard the firing. We'll be outnumbered three to one. We'd better get out of here."

By mid-morning all of the surviving Double Circle hands were back in their hideout except for Blaine, who had been taken to town and left in the keeping of the doctor. The two Spearhead prisoners had been hanged at daylight. Jackson had been reluctant to take that course of action, but the men were adamant. They argued that they had lost one of their comrades, the Spearhead riders were nothing but a bunch of hard cases gathered by Decker for the purpose of killing and rustling, and they had been blatantly stealing land and cattle from Double Circle and Flying V. Moreover, they had burned the Double Circle headquarters.

"Don't think they wouldn't hang any of us if they caught us," argued Jerome.

The two captives were hanged along the trail that led from Spearhead to town. The riders of Double Circle were sending a message.

All and all it had been a good night's work, thought Jackson. They had wiped out a good portion of Spearhead's crew, losing only one man in the process.

CHAPTER 10

At Spearhead headquarters Treadwell laid his hard words on Decker.

"Can't blame me," asserted Decker in his own defense. "I wasn't even with them. I had my part of the crew clear on the other side of the range."

"Why'd you split up your crew? It was a fool thing to do. They would never have attacked if the crew had all been together. You just keep letting them make a sucker out of you, Decker. Not only that, I think you've been lying to me."

Decker's neck and face went a hot red. "What's that supposed to mean, Graham?"

"It means you throw two men down a thirteen-hundred foot hole and a week later they turn up alive like they were Lazarus."

"How was I supposed to know the shaft had filled up with water?"

"You're supposed to know, Decker. You're not thorough enough. Before you throw a man in a pit, you'd better make sure he's dead. The pit is just a place to throw a dead body so nobody finds it. The problem is you enjoy this too much. You enjoy hurting people. You can't just kill a man and then throw him down a shaft; you want him to be alive, screaming and praying all the way down. If you worried as much about doing your job as you do about making people suffer, maybe I could count on you to do something right."

Decker had no defense for this, so he raged inwardly but held his tongue. He turned away and muttered, "I'll be going to bed."

"You're not thinking of taking the crew out again tomorrow are you?"

"Thought that was what you wanted," said Decker without turning around.

"Not now. I have a better plan."

Decker turned around, his face a grim mask. "What's that?"

"Last week I sent a telegram to the governor. I got a reply

yesterday. The governor's coming. He wants to speak to me personally. That can only mean . . . well, it's something good. The governor and I have gotten to be pretty good friends and I'll have his ear while he's here. I'll tell him how Double Circle has hired gunmen like Colin McGrath, ambushed and killed a whole crew of my men—hanged two of them and shot the rest. I'll tell him how they're a pack of rustlers and they started a range war. By the time he leaves here, Jackson and McGrath and their whole crew will have prices on their heads and U.S. marshals after them. They'll either wind up in jail or hanged. This is how things work when you use your head, Decker."

Decker started to turn away again, but he stopped and said, "Since we're not going to be out huntin' Double Circle tomorrow, how about givin' me and the crew the day off? We need a rest."

"I don't pay any of you to take a day off in the middle of the week, Decker."

The territorial governor sat in a chair in the sheriff's office and Graham Treadwell sat across from him, regaling him in fine detail with a fabricated story of Double Circle's atrocities. When he was finished the governor said, "And you say it was this Frank Jackson who did these things?"

"Jackson and his hired gunman, Colin McGrath. He's the gunslick who murdered a man named Mustin in cold blood."

"Mmmm," said the governor, stroking his chin. "That's not how I heard that story."

"Well, stories have a way of getting distorted in the telling."

"Yes," said the governor, "they certainly do."

"In any case," said Treadwell, "I'm certain I can count on you, Sir, to help us see that justice is done here in the valley."

"I shall make very attempt to do so," said the governor.

"Thank you. On another subject; about my plans to campaign for . . ."

The governor held up a hand. "Not now. We can talk about that later. Meanwhile I want to have a meeting. I want you there and I want your foreman there. What's his name?"

"Decker."

"I want Mr. Decker there. I will invite some other people of my own choosing. I plan to get to the bottom of this."

It was as if a shadow had come over Treadwell's face. "At the bottom of it, Sir? I've just told you what's been happening here. I had assumed that my word would be sufficient to . . ."

"Wouldn't you agree, Graham," cut in the governor, "that in affairs of this nature a man in my position would be remiss if he did not delve into every aspect of the situation?"

"Of course, Sir, I was merely . . ."

"Good, then we'll leave it at that until tomorrow. Ten o'clock in the morning. Now, where is a good place for a meeting like this?"

"Here in the courthouse would . . ."

The governor shook his head. "Too formal."

"Well, there are three churches in town."

"Definitely not a church. There may be some swearing."

"That only leaves a saloon," said Treadwell.

"Perfect. Which one?"

"Bull's Horn. Across from the hotel. I'll arrange it."

"I'll see you there at ten o'clock tomorrow morning."

The governor was a true politician, and he liked an audience. That afternoon he instructed his aides to spread the news of the meeting and tell people that on the morrow, their governor, a man as wise as Solomon of old, would bring peace and justice to this place.

From the beginning he had wanted the meeting to be held in a saloon and had manipulated Treadwell into suggesting it. The governor was certain the room would be packed, and he wanted it to be packed with voters. Women did not vote, so he did not want them there. Women—decent ones at least—did not enter saloons, so . . . the problem was solved.

The governor was a tall man in his sixties. He had been somewhat handsome as a younger man and now, with partial greying of his hair and moustache, he looked distinguished. He always carried a cane, though he suffered from no physical malady that would require him to do so, and he kept himself impeccably groomed and dressed.

He had invited the town marshal and the county sheriff to be present; the sheriff because this county was his jurisdiction, the marshal out of courtesy. He had asked them to help keep order in the group.

As the governor had predicted, the room was packed. He had ordered that no liquor be sold until the meeting was concluded. He wanted his listeners to be sober.

Frank Jackson and Colin McGrath stood at the back of the room, where they could keep their backs to the wall. They had taken a risk even coming to town today, but their reason for being here was obvious.

By way of introduction, the governor said, "There was a time when this great territory was not yet even a part of the United States. Indians and buffalo roamed these lands. White men were outsiders and came here at their own risk. There were trappers, prospectors, buffalo hunters, and others. Settlers came, the railroad was built, telegraph lines were strung. This is a civilized country now. And we are expected to act like we are a part of it if we ever expect to achieve statehood. People are watching us: easterners, politicians in Washington. We can no longer do as we please and expect no consequences. Too long has the gun been the law here. Now we need the law to start being the law. This meeting is not an official meeting. It's highly unorthodox. It is not considered to be the job of the territorial governor to be an arbitrator of disputes between ranchers. I am here out of a desire to be of service to a good friend."

Graham Treadwell smiled benevolently and gave a slight bow of the head.

The governor continued, "I've heard two stories. One has been told to me by the owner of the Spearhead ranch, the other—a very different tale—by the owner of the Double Circle. If I'm to believe Mr. Treadwell, Mr. Jackson and his crew are scoundrels, cattle thieves, and murderers. If I'm to believe Mr. Jackson, those things are true of Mr. Treadwell and his crew. I have also heard the story of another rancher who was accused of murder but was found not guilty by a jury. One story has it that he was framed, that he did not commit the murder. The other story has it that he was guilty, but misguided jurors believed him to be innocent."

"Governor, it sounds like you need a tie breaker," came a voice from the back of the room. The crowd erupted in laughter.

The governor laughed too and then raised his hand for silence, "That's exactly what I need, my friends. Would anyone like to come forward? And I need someone who is not employed and never has been employed by either of the ranches in question."

A low rumble of murmuring came from the crowd, but no one spoke up.

"Surely there's someone," said the governor.

Then a voice came from the back of the room. There were various reactions from the assemblage: approval, disapproval, derision, friendly laughter. The crowd parted as Tom Lee Maryann moved through it and came forward to stand in front of the governor. The governor wore his politician's benevolent smile. He started to speak. "And you, Sir . . ." He stopped. The smile went away, replaced by a look of astonishment.

He started to say something, but Treadwell interrupted him, "Sir, I protest. This man . . ."

The governor cut him off, his affability completely gone. He looked at Treadwell and said coldly, "I'll ask you, Sir, to be silent while this man speaks." Then, with a look of infinite kindness, he said to Tom Lee, "Tell me, Sir, what have you to say?"

Tom Lee told about the obvious frame-up of Vince Hamm, of the bird droppings on the saddle. He told about seeing Ty Decker ride up to the back entrance of the Crazy Horse with another man who was walking, leading a horse with a man strapped over the saddle, and carry that man inside, later emerging without him. He said, "I didn't know who it was. I didn't know he wasn't dead. I figured they had killed somebody and tossed him down a shaft."

"Every few days," he continued, "at night, Spearhead riders bring in a herd to the loading pens and load them up. If you go down and look you'll find Double Circle and Flying V brands on most of those cattle. They're shipped off to the east. I don't know where they go."

"Sir," burst out Treadwell, "surely you're not going to believe this man. He is a disgusting drunk. You can't trust anything he says."

The governor turned to face Treadwell and the look on his face brought complete silence to the assemblage. He said, "I would trust this man with my life, Sir. Then he added in a voice so low that only those in the front of the group could understand the words, "In fact, I have."

He took in a deep breath, raised his head, and said, "I've heard everything I need to hear, Gentlemen. Thank you all for being here." Then he said, "I would like Frank Jackson, Graham Treadwell, and Sheriff Wardman to meet me directly in the sheriff's office."

When the five men were gathered in Sheriff Wardman's office, the governor said, "The situation, Gentlemen, is quite clear to me." Turning to Treadwell he said, "Mr. Treadwell, I believe you are a scoundrel and a blackguard. It's pretty evident that you are a murderer, a liar, and a cattle thief. I will leave it to Sheriff Wardman to determine what to do about these things. Meanwhile I strongly recommend that you cease and desist your nefarious activities."

Treadwell's face reddened. He rose to his feet and said, "You can never prove a single one of those accusations."

"Maybe not," said the governor, "but I will tell you this, Sir. If I were you, I would abandon any thoughts of a political career in this state or any other. I will personally see to that."

Treadwell turned on his heel and stomped out of the room. When he was gone, the governor said to Jackson, "Frank, why didn't you tell me about Ben?"

"I would have eventually. But I wanted to give him the chance to do it first."

They gazed at each other momentarily and the governor shook his head. "Too bad. Too bad about him, too bad about his family."

Then he said, "Well, Gentlemen, I'm dry. Let's go back over to the saloon."

In the saloon the governor was once again the center of attention and, being a politician, he had no objection to this. After ordering a beer he said, "Gentlemen, I think you all have a right to hear what I'm about to say. When I said I was here to help a good friend, I was not referring to Mr. Treadwell as he assumed I was. I was referring to Frank Jackson. Captain Jackson, and I and another man, whose name was Benjamin Wallace, were soldiers together in the United States Army under General Winfield Scott, during the Mexican War."

A wistful look came onto the governor's face. "Ah, Gentlemen, we were friends as only soldiers in war can be friends." He took a drink of beer, pulled a handkerchief from his pocket, and wiped his mouth and perfectly trimmed mustache. Something about his face and his stance told the men they were about to hear a story. And his words and slightly theatrical tone, when he began speaking, confirmed it.

"September 8, 1847. Not many people know that date, not many people remember it. But those of us who were there will never forget it. Over eight-hundred American soldiers lost their lives that day, along with many fine young Mexican soldiers—all fighting men, all deserving of honor.

"It was near Mexico City, which, you may know, is a long way from home for an American. It was in a place known as El Molino Del Rey—the king's mill. All in all there must have been fifteen-thousand men on both sides who fought in that battle. We fought most of the morning just to break through the gates and then we had to fight room to room for at least two hours. Those Mexican boys were fierce and bold fighters, and I fell wounded, hit with a musket ball. I was sitting there, leaning against a wall with dead men all around me, unable to move. The Mexicans rallied and counter-attacked. They were coming toward me, and I don't mind telling you, Gentlemen, I had commended my soul to my maker. But something happened right then: A man appeared, standing directly over me, interposing himself between me and those Mexicans. He had a pistol in each hand and for just a moment, blazing away, he held those Mexicans off. When his pistols were both empty he turned to me and said, 'Major, We're going to Kingdom Come, but we're going together.'"

The room was silent. The governor took another swig of beer, wiped his mouth and moustache again, and surveyed the room, allowing the suspense to draw out. Finally he said, "Those Mexicans charged with their bayonets fixed and into the middle of this came Frank Jackson on horseback, leading a squadron of the 2nd Dragoons. They were outnumbered three to one, but they fought like tigers. Not one of us left the battlefield that day without wounds, but we're still here to tell about it. And the man who stood over me with his pistols blazing, the man who saved my life, the man Frank Jackson and I knew as Benjamin Wallace, is the man you know as Tom Lee Maryann."

There was a silence broken only by a few low, approving comments from the listeners, and then one of the men nearest the governor asked, "Why did he change his name?"

The governor exchanged a look with Jackson, and Jackson gave a faint shake of the head. The governor looked back at the questioner and said, "I guess you'd have to ask him that."

The governor left the next morning and Jackson went to see him off.

The governor said, "Let's walk, Captain. I like to walk while I talk."

"I remember that about you, Major."

They walked alongside the train tracks, passing the cars one by one, passing the engine. The governor said, "I'm taking Ben with me. He's agreed to come and live with me and Margaret, at least for a while. And," he added with significance in his tone, "it probably will be just a while."

"You mean?"

"I spoke with the doctor. It's alcoholic liver disease. He won't live much longer. But we'll see that he has a good life as long as it lasts."

"Will you try to get him to stop drinking?"

There was sadness in the governor's smile. "I guess that'll be up to him, but I don't really think there's much point in it. I hope you don't take this the wrong way, but I think it'll be a mercy when he dies."

Jackson nodded soberly.

"I looked for him," said the governor. "I sent letters and telegrams . . ."

"So did I. Nobody seemed to know where he'd gone."

"I wish I'd known sooner, so I could have gone to the funeral."

They walked in contemplative silence for a few minutes and then the governor said, "I'll never forget Mexico, Frank. You and Ben . . ."

"None of us will ever forget it," said Jackson.

They had gotten some distance away from the train and now they turned and started back.

"Pretty country," said the governor.

Jackson nodded.

The governor said, "Frank, there's something I never told you about that day at Molino Del Rey." He looked away and they walked without speaking for so long a time that Jackson thought the governor was not going to finish what he had started to say.

But finally, he said, "I was terrified. Worse than terrified. I've never told this to anyone else, not even Margaret."

Jackson said nothing. They walked and he waited, knowing there was more.

"A man can take a bullet or musket ball, Frank. It kills him or it doesn't. I had one in me already . . . but those Mexicans were coming. I was on the ground, my guns were empty, and I couldn't move. You know what they would have done to me."

"They would've used their bayonets."

The governor nodded. "It's a fear I've had since I was a boy. The thought of a bayonet being shoved through my body has always been . . ." his voice fell off. He shook his head. After a pause he said in a soft, low voice, "And suddenly there was Ben; standing over me, a pistol in each hand, blazing away, screaming at those Mexicans like he was Sampson killing Philistines. They shot him three times, you know, before you rode in with your men and drove them back."

"I know."

"I wanted to tell you, Frank, that . . ." He stopped speaking, paused for a moment, then turned to Jackson and looked him squarely in the eyes, "I just wanted you to know I haven't forgotten that day . . . and never will."

It was Sunday and the restaurant was closed. Jackson rode to Bonnie's place and was pleased to find McGrath there playing cards with Bonnie and Ruth. Lyssa was sitting contentedly on his lap. Jackson took a seat at the table and Bonnie patted his arm and said, "Is the governor gone?"

"Yes. He took Tom Lee, you know."

"Yes, I know. Tom Lee came over to say goodbye to us."

Jackson noticed that Ruth's eyes were red and he knew she had been crying. A small tear rolled out and he reached over and gently touched her hand and said, "Is this about Tom Lee?"

She nodded.

"You grew kind of attached to him, didn't you?"

She nodded again.

Bonnie said, "Colin told us the story. He said you and the governor call Tom Lee by another name."

"His name is Benjamin Wallace."

"Why did he change it?"

A sad smile came onto Jackson's face. "A few years ago I received word that Ben's entire family—his wife, two sons, and a daughter—had died in a cholera outbreak. I didn't learn about it until a few weeks afterward. I tried to contact him, but no one knew where he was. They said that after the funeral he just disappeared."

"And the name," said Ruth, "His family?"

"Yes. The boys were named Tom and Lee, the daughter was Mary, and his wife was named Ann. I knew her. She was a good and kind woman."

Ruth rose and left the room and it was a long time before she came back.

Perry Strickland was popular among the other miners and when he told his friends where he'd been and the story of his and McGrath's and Jackson's escape from the mine, their desire for retribution against Decker and Treadwell was a fearsome thing.

A few nights later, one of the miners saw eight Spearhead horses tied outside one of the saloons. He and Strickland gathered a large group of miners who armed themselves with firearms and clubs and went into the saloon, disarmed the Spearhead hard cases, and carried them to a train which was waiting on a siding.

They put their captives in an empty boxcar and closed and barred the door. They then took up a collection and paid the conductor a healthy sum to see that the men were not released until the train reached California. Spearhead's numbers had just dropped by eight men.

The miners went to their favorite saloon and celebrated their accomplishment as drinking men generally do. Early the next morning, a large group of them went to Treadwell's town site, pulled up all the iron stakes—numbering in the hundreds—and amassed them in a great pile in the center of what would have been the town's main street.

Even before the governor had invited Frank Jackson, Graham Treadwell, and the sheriff to the meeting in the sheriff's office, Decker had already guessed what the governor had decided. During the meeting at the Bull's horn, it had become clear to Decker that Treadwell had fallen out of favor with the governor, and now all the reasons Decker had ever had for remaining in Treadwell's employ were gone.

The bulk of the Spearhead crew had either been killed by Jackson's crew the night of the fight in the canyon or shipped by train to California, and of the few who remained most had deserted, no longer liking the odds. As a fighting ranch, Spearhead was finished. Moreover, Treadwell's political career was ended before it had begun, and any respect Decker had had for the man had long ago disappeared.

He pulled his dusty war bag out from under his bunk and said to Robart, who was watching him do it, "I'm leavin'."

"Guessed that," said Robart. "I'll go with you."

Decker stopped what he was doing and looked at Robart. "Before I go, I'm going to kill McGrath."

Robart's head nodded faintly for a few moments and he said, "Why not?"

The door of Frank Jackson's former office burst open and Carol rushed in. "I've found him. I know where Father is."

"Where?" Mandy asked excitedly.

"You remember Agnes Corgway. She went west on a trip and on the way back she stopped in a little town. She was eating at a restaurant and she picked up a newspaper someone had left. The newspaper talked about a range war and one Frank Jackson who was involved in it."

"A range war?" exclaimed her two siblings.

John, the oldest son, said, "Can't be Father."

"Jackson is a pretty common name," Remarked Mandy, her excitement gone.

"That's what Agnes thought, so she talked to one of the locals and they described Frank Jackson. It's our father. He's gone and gotten himself into a range war."

Mandy walked around the room, wringing her hands. "Oh that foolish, foolish man. What is he trying to do?"

"Well," said Carol, "We have to go get him. We've got to bring him home before something bad happens to him."

Sheriff Wardman had no real evidence against Treadwell, but there were plenty of people who were willing to testify against Decker. The problem was Decker had disappeared. That was fine with the sheriff. Decker was a snake, and he had not relished the thought of bracing the man. As long as he was gone and stayed gone the sheriff wouldn't worry about it. The range war was over, and even if Treadwell had wanted to continue it, there were not enough men left on Spearhead to make it feasible.

Wardman knew the other ranchers in the area were taking back what they believed was rightfully theirs in the way of livestock, and he made no attempt to intervene. Hopefully they would do so peaceably and he would not have to get involved.

Frank Jackson had a pretty good idea of the number of Double Circle cattle Spearhead had stolen and, there being no one to stop them now, he, McGrath, and the rest of the Double Circle crew rode on Spearhead's range with impunity, paying no attention to brands, and went to work replacing the lost herd. Vince Hamm was doing the same down at his end of the range.

It was a pleasant evening and Frank and Bonnie had decided to go for a ride. Ordinarily talk flowed freely between the two, but this evening Bonnie could tell that something was on Frank's mind.

Presently he turned to her and said, "When my wife died, I swore I would never marry again. I was sure I could never love another woman. I don't know if you felt that way when your husband died."

"I swore I'd never marry again after I'd been with him for two weeks. I swore at myself for having married him in the first place."

He smiled faintly and looked away. "I had heard you felt that way. I was just checking."

"Hmph," she said, "If you'd given up that easily when you were inside that mine, you'd still be there."

He turned to look at her in bewilderment. "I'm not sure I understand," he said.

"Not very romantic, are you?"

"Actually I am."

"Then maybe you should act like it."

He tried to hold her eyes, to fathom her meaning, or at least to determine if it was what he thought it was, but she looked away, giving him nothing more. It was up to him now to take a chance. Well, he thought, taking chances was all he had been doing since he had come to this place. But this one somehow seemed more frightening than any of the others.

They rode in silence for a time and then he said, "All I can tell you, Bonnie, is that I love you."

She reined in her horse and he did the same. She turned to look at him, and her eyes were wet. "I love you too, Frank. And I want you to know that it's the first time I've ever loved a man. I'm not a girl anymore, but a heart is a fragile thing at any age. Please Frank, take good care of mine."

Jake Treadwell was furious with his father for locking Hughey in his room and had refused to speak to him since he had done so. He was made to sleep in the bunkhouse with the men and was allowed no contact with his brother. Treadwell took Hughey his meals and anything else he needed, keeping the key to the room in his pocket.

Treadwell had not allowed Jake to ride with his crew of hard cases when they were seeking a showdown with the Double Circle crew. Jake was fifteen-years-old and had no experience with gunfighting. On these occasions Treadwell either made the boy stay at home and work with the blacksmith, shoeing horses, or sent him to some other part of the range where there would be no action. Therefore, Jake had not been in the same danger as the rest of the crew these last few weeks.

But things were falling apart at the ranch, he could tell. Most of the crew was gone, and the handful of men that remained was disheartened and rebellious. It seemed like every time he looked, Spearhead had fewer riders. Ty Decker had become sullen and uncommunicative, and he seemed to have lost control of the men. And, what was more frightening to Jake, Treadwell seemed to have lost control of Decker.

Jake had never liked Decker and he didn't like the kind of men Decker had hired. He remembered the old crew before Decker had started employing hard cases. Those men had all been his friends. They were honest, hardworking cow punchers. Since his earliest years Jake had looked forward to someday becoming the foreman of Spearhead. Now, he no longer cared about that. Hughey was more important to him than anything else. As far as Jake was concerned, his half-brother was his only family.

One night, when Treadwell was gone to town, Jake took an axe from the woodshed, carried it into the house and up the stairs. He knocked on the door and said, "Hughey, stand back. I'm bustin' you out." He began swinging the axe.

Alarmed by the noise, the cook came running upstairs with a rifle. Jake said to him, "George, I don't want any trouble. I'm takin' my brother out of here."

With a solemn expression George said, "Good for you Jake. I always did like you."

"I'm sorry about this George, but by not trying to stop me you're makin' it so you'll have to leave too. Pa will never let you stay after this."

"Jake, a man's got to do the right thing. That's somethin' you've learnt and your pa never will. I've been plannin' on leaving this place for a while. Been workin' here for three years and that's just three years longer than any man ought to have to work for Graham Treadwell. You just helped me make my move. Good luck to you boys."

"Good luck to you too, George. Hope to see you again someday."

Jake had readied two saddle horses along with a pack horse laden with supplies, and the two boys were soon in the saddle and away from ranch headquarters. Hughey said, "Where we goin', Jake?"

"Campin', I guess. Up on Silent Mountain."

"Can we go up to Canyon Mouth first? There's some people up there that I think will be worried about me. I'd like to let them know I'm alright."

"Sure we can, Hughey. And will you whack up a tune on that piano for me? I've kinda been wantin' to hear you play."

CHAPTER 11

There was a restlessness in McGrath that he could not identify, a sense of something left unfinished. He was lonely—he knew that—but he had been lonely for a long time, and it was something he bore, not knowing what else to do. But this restlessness rode him and wore on him, sometimes turning him sullen and quiet.

It was Saturday night and McGrath, as usual, had gone to play cards with Bonnie and Ruth and Frank Jackson. But he had been unable to keep his mind on the game and after a brief time had excused himself and had gone out and tramped over to the saloon, leaving his three friends bewildered.

"Wonder what's eatin' him?" said Jackson.

Bonnie looked at Ruth and could see that, though the young woman was trying to hide it, she was hurt.

"Who knows?" said Bonnie. "You men can be moody creatures."

"You're thinking of your first husband," jibed Jackson.

"My first husband wasn't moody," said Bonnie. "He was very even tempered—always mean."

McGrath went over to his usual saloon and ordered a beer. In truth, he didn't feel like drinking. He didn't feel like doing anything. He tried to think of Ruth. He wanted to think of Ruth. He knew he wanted to be with her, but when he thought of going back over to where she was, the restless feeling stopped him.

He finished his beer and put the mug down and stepped outside. The restlessness had made him alert and he was suddenly aware of a man standing in the shadows between two buildings, a gray blur in the dim light. He could smell the smoke wafting from the man's cigarette. The man seemed to be aware of his scrutiny and moved farther back into the shadows.

Why would he do that? Why was he there in the first place?

At this time of night McGrath would never walk in that direction. He would go the opposite way. If the man was waiting for him, why was he in that particular spot? It could only be because he wasn't alone. If there was someone else, he would have to be somewhere in the opposite direction in order to box McGrath in.

Acutely alert, all of his senses heightened, McGrath feigned disinterest. He leaned indolently back against the saloon wall and rolled a smoke. After a few drags on the cigarette, he flicked it into the street and casually turned and strolled back into the barroom. Once inside he ran around the corner of the bar, into the back room and out the back door.

Decker watched as McGrath smoked a cigarette in front of the saloon and then went back inside. Why had the man done that? It didn't seem normal. Decker hated McGrath, hated him more than he had ever hated another human being, and he blamed the man for everything that had gone wrong; blamed him for the demise of all his hopes and aspirations. McGrath had beaten him and humiliated him and frustrated him in a hundred ways. And more than he had ever wanted anything in his life, Ty Decker wanted Colin McGrath dead.

Decker lived by no code. There was no honor in him. Avarice and malice had long ago displaced any goodness he had ever possessed. He could face a man in a fist fight or a gun fight and had done so more than once in his life, but he would much rather back-shoot a man than run the risk entailed in a face-to-face contest. He always liked to keep the odds on his side.

And so when McGrath threw away his cigarette and went back inside the saloon, Decker crossed the distance at a run and looked into the bar room. It was as he had feared: McGrath was not there. He motioned to Robart to come out of the shadows and the two men ran between two buildings and down an alley to where they had left their horses. McGrath had outsmarted him too many times for Decker to ever underestimate the man, and right now the last thing in the world he wanted was to be hunted by the man. As he swung up into the saddle, a voice came from the shadows and Decker knew instantly who it was.

"Were you going to leave without saying goodbye?" McGrath stepped out of the darkness. Decker had his pistol in his hand. He swung it toward McGrath, shouting a curse.

As he fell from the saddle, Decker did not even realize that he had been shot. He never would.

Robart flung his hands in the air, sending his pistol flying. "Don't shoot me, McGrath."

McGrath said, "Are you finished here?"

"I'm leavin', McGrath, right now."

"That's good thinkin'. Don't ever come back."

"Not me. I've got no grudge against you anyhow." And with that, Robart reined his horse around and pounded away into the night.

Sheriff Wardman was relieved when he learned of Ty Decker's death. He had always feared the man. He personally took the body out to Spearhead, deriving a certain pleasure from being the one to tell Treadwell his foreman was dead.

Treadwell showed no emotion and made no comment other than to say, "You've done your job, now get off my land."

"Looks like your fangs have been drawn, Treadwell." The sheriff turned his horse and rode back to town.

Treadwell had one of his men bury Decker's body. There was no service, no words were spoken over the grave, and it wasn't until the next day that it occurred to him to send word to Decker's mother that her son had been killed and buried.

Decker's mother stood in the open doorway, stunned, watching as Treadwell's messenger rode away. She and her son had not been close. In fact, during most of his life they had disliked each other. And now with his death there came to her a sense of freedom, which overrode any feelings of grief. She had been released from prison. There was nothing to keep her here a minute longer.

She had money, a lot of it. Treadwell had paid her well to do this odious job and there had never been an opportunity to spend any of it. She had been imprisoned here along with her charge. She gathered up her meager possessions, put on her hat, and stepped outside. She took a last, long look at the garden she had so carefully tended through the years—the only thing about this place that mattered at all to her—and then turned away.

There was a decrepit buggy in a shed near the house, but no horse. She would have to walk. She didn't mind that. She would not have minded if she had had to crawl away from this place, as long as she got away. At the last moment it occurred to her that the woman was still locked in her room. What would happen to her? Decker had brought supplies just two days before. It would be nearly a week before Treadwell sent someone out with more. By then the woman would probably be dead.

It was a close-run thing, but there was just enough compassion in Decker's mother for this woman to whose needs she had attended for eight years, to impel her to go back in and unlock the door of the room.

The woman was on her bed reading. She looked up, and Decker's mother said in a flat tone, "It's over. I'm leaving." And she left the door open and walked away.

The woman came out and looked around. She went in to where the supplies were kept and found something to eat, at once savoring and fearing the freedom she had so abruptly been given. She did not leave the house right away, having nowhere to go and being unprepared to plan a new life. There were plenty of provisions left and she consumed them sparingly, allowing herself a smaller daily ration than Decker's mother had allotted her, mentally preparing herself for the time when she would be forced by necessity to leave this place: this place she detested, but to which she felt inexplicably and illogically bound.

For the first few days after Decker's death, Treadwell stayed in the house most of the time, pacing restlessly, drinking heavily, eating little, sleeping almost not at all, and fuming with a seething hatred at the governor, at Decker, at his two sons and his cook for deserting him, at McGrath, but mostly at Frank Jackson. He spent days in the most intense state of mental concentration, attempting to formulate a new plan—one that would restore to him everything he had lost.

A steady parade of ideas passed through his mind, ideas involving ways to discredit the governor in the public eye and resurrect his, Treadwell's, chances of a political career. He would hire a new foreman and a new crew, tougher men than the last foreman and crew—men who could destroy McGrath and Jackson.

But in every plan there was at least one fatal flaw, and, fantasize though he may, Treadwell could not come up with a suitable plan. After days of this he finally accepted the fact that it was all over. He would never have a political career; never own the largest ranch in the state. These things were lost forever, and the knowledge was a bitter gall to him.

When he finally emerged from the darkness of his empty house, bearded, haggard, pale; blinking his eyes against the bright, unaccustomed sunlight; his hostler, one of the few people left on the ranch, after having saddled a horse for his boss and watched him ride out, remarked to himself, "He's aged twenty years in a week."

Treadwell rode directly to his town site, the town that would bear his name, the one dream left to him. This could still become a reality. History would not record his crimes. No charges had been brought against him, nor would they be. Those things would be forgotten. But his name would live on in his town. A few years from now it would be a large and blossoming city. People from all over the world would visit here to see what he had created and what it had grown into. Libraries would be named after him; hospitals, schools, and public buildings would all bear his name.

These were his thoughts as he rode onto his town site. And then, as abruptly as if he had been struck in the face, he jerked the reins. There was something that had not been here last time he had come. Who had done this? Who had come and profaned his town site?

It was a large dark mound, unidentifiable at this distance. He kicked the horse into a run and as he approached the mound, he recognized what it was. At first he wondered for just a fleeting second who had brought so many iron stakes and piled them here. And then he understood.

He reined the horse savagely around, turning in a complete circle, scanning the entire area. He had paid thousands of dollars for this survey, thousands of dollars to have these stakes driven and have his town, its streets and blocks and building sites, laid out. Who would do such a thing and why?

The answer was not long in coming. Treadwell was not the kind of man to accept his own guilt, but he knew who it was that had the greatest reason to hate him. He gave a great bellow of rage, and viciously spurred the horse away from this empty, featureless piece of land.

For a man who was in the habit of planning his every move, what Treadwell was about to do was uncharacteristic, and yet, considering the circumstances, quite predictable. Nothing mattered anymore except one thing and his thoughts all centered on that. And the white-hot wrath inside him made him spur his horse without mercy. He possessed a malignant soul and a killing lust was upon him now. All other things were less important.

He rode into town from the east side, slowing the lathered horse as he did, passing the various saloons frequented by the miners. He pulled his carbine out of the saddle boot and levered in a cartridge.

He was prepared to wait however long it took for Frank Jackson to arrive in town, but as it turned out, Jackson was already there, having come in to visit his wounded puncher as he did every evening. Treadwell saw him come out of the restaurant and start across the street on his way to the doctor's house. Treadwell stepped out of the saddle, dropped the reins, raised the carbine, and fired.

Jackson heard the shot and knew it was intended for him. He was in the middle of the street, and he bolted to the other side, where a horse was tied, using it for cover. Treadwell levered in another cartridge and shot the horse. The animal dropped to the ground and Jackson dropped down behind it, shielded partially by the horse and partially by a tar barrel.

Walking forward, Treadwell was levering in cartridges and firing as he advanced, taking no time to aim, speaking emphatic curses, as if he were saying them to himself, repeating Frank Jackson's name over and over as though it were an epithet.

As he passed the marshal's office, Marshal Croft stepped out, holding a rifle. "Here now, Graham, stop that." Treadwell swung his rifle in an almost casual manner and fired. The marshal was knocked backward by the bullet, landing on the floor, half in, half out of his office.

Jackson had his pistol out, but the distance was too great for pistol accuracy. At the rate Treadwell was firing, he would soon be out of bullets. Jackson was too clear-headed to engage in a stand up fight at rifle range, armed only with a pistol. So he decided to wait for Treadwell to either close the distance or expend all his cartridges. Repeatedly, Treadwell's shots hit the horse's carcass or passed overhead. Jackson waited. When at last he heard the hammer of the carbine click down on the empty bullet chamber, he stood up.

Treadwell was closer now. He dropped the carbine and pulled his pistol. Jackson was taking careful aim and, seeing this, Treadwell snapped off a shot that grazed Jackson's upper arm. Jackson's shot hit Treadwell high up on the right side of the chest and spun him around. As he fell, he dropped his pistol, but when he heard Jackson's running boots approaching he rolled over and reached for it, cursing. Jackson's boot landed on Treadwell's hand and Jackson reached down and wrenched the pistol from the man's grasp.

Up on Silent Mountain, the two boys had just finished breakfast when Jake spotted approaching dust in the distance. "Hand me the field glasses, will you Hughey?" He watched through the glasses for a few minutes and then said, "It's George. Does he know you come up here?"

"Sure, I've told him."

Jake stepped out in the open and gave their former cook a halloo and a wave and the old man waved back. It was a hard trail and it was nearly an hour later when George finally rode into camp.

Hughey said, "Get down, George, and have some breakfast."

"I'll do that, boys, but first I got to tell you somethin'. Your Pa was in a gun fight. He's shot."

"How bad?" asked Jake, tonelessly.

"He'll live, but he killed the marshal so he'll hang." George walked over to the fire and lifted the coffee pot off the coals and poured himself a cup. "Did I smell bacon?"

"We ate it all," said Hughey. Seeing George's disappointment, he forced a smile and said, "I can fry up some more."

Jake stood staring off in the distance toward the ranch. From where he stood he could see much of Spearhead and parts of Flying V and Double Circle. At last he turned and walked over and sat on a rock across from George.

George said, "The ranch belongs to you boys now. You'll have to run it."

"Not me," said Hughey. "It's Jake's ranch."

Ever loyal, Jake said, "No Hughey, both of us fifty-fifty. It will always be that way."

"You know I'm not a rancher, Jake, and I don't ever want to be."

"Don't expect you to," said Jake, "but you still own half."

"You boys can work that out later," said George. "We ain't got much of a crew left and if you'll take my advice you'll fire everybody except Jack and Skid. There'll be plenty of good riders comin' round lookin' for work now that your Pa is gone."

"And you, George, will you come back?" asked Jake.

George grinned hugely, "Try and stop me."

Jake was only fifteen, but as George watched him he seemed to see the weight of Spearhead settling on those young shoulders. Jake didn't want this, but he'd do it. George knew that about the young man.

Hughey said, "Jake, we'd better ride over to Double Circle and down to Flying V, talk to Jackson and Hamm and tell 'em things are going to be different. Spearhead ain't their enemy anymore."

Jake nodded, "Yeah, we need to do that."

George headed back to Spearhead while the boys broke camp and packed up their supplies.

Halfway to the ranch Jake and Hughey saw a woman walking alone, far from any house or road. They looked at each other in bewilderment and rode toward her. Seeing them approach, she stopped. She looked frightened. She looked around as though seeking a place to hide.

Drawing near, Jake said, "Ma'am, is there anything we can do for you?" Seeing the fear on her face he said, "Ma'am, there's no need to be afraid. My name's Jake Treadwell, and this is my brother Hughey."

Her eyes grew wide and a little cry escaped her throat and then Jake thought he recognized her—but it couldn't be. That woman was dead.

"Did you say, Hughey?" she choked.

"Yes," said Jake.

And when she began to sob, Jake knew.

She went over to Hughey, holding her hand on her mouth, attempting to control herself. She touched him on the leg and reached up and gently touched his hand. A sob escaped her throat. She could see that Hughey didn't understand. Suddenly, something came into his eyes. He turned to Jake and Jake nodded and said, "Yes, Hughey."

Hughey slid off the horse and threw himself into his mother's arms. "They told me you were dead." He sobbed. "Where have you been? They told me you were dead."

Her legs grew weak and she dropped to her knees, and Hughey knelt in front of her, gently holding her. Jake turned away. His eyes were wet, but he was smiling.

The letter finally arrived from California. One of Ruth's letters had found its way to the right person. She knew what it was, and she took it back to the restaurant, unopened.

Bonnie saw Ruth's face and asked, "What's wrong?"

Ruth looked down at the letter in her hand, drawing Bonnie's gaze there as well.

Bonnie sucked in her breath and the two women looked at each other for a long, fearful moment.

Finally Bonnie said, with a trembling voice, "Let's get it over with."

The letter read,

Dear Mrs. Moreland,

My wife and I were very sorry to learn of the death of your husband. You have our deepest sympathy. We now understand why you did not rejoin the wagon company that night. I regret to inform you that Mrs. Meier died on the same day as your husband, leaving Lyssa an orphan. My wife was with the poor woman when she died. She asked for her child, but as you know, you and your husband had not arrived. Mrs. Meier told my wife that it was her wish that you should raise the child. She asked that her wagon and goods be sold and the money be given to you for the purpose of the keeping of the girl. If you will send me the information, I shall make sure the money is gotten to your bank. If you should wish to complete the journey that you and your husband started, please come to where we are at. You and the girl can lodge with us as long as is needful. The weather is beautiful here and the soil is fertile. They tell us they grow things all year round as there is no snow or very cold weather. But you must hurry if you want to make your place here. It is growing quite fast. More people arrive every day.
Sincerely,
Albert Day

After the gunfight with Decker, McGrath threw himself into the ranch work, driving himself from daylight until suppertime, often going out afterward in the dark to do something that could have waited until morning. Moreover, he tended to be uncommunicative and irritable.

Observing this, Jackson held his tongue until finally one evening he said to McGrath, "Colin, you need to go to town."

Perplexed, McGrath said, "What for?"

"That's for you to figure out. Sometimes a man can think too much and do too little. Some things you have to just do and stop thinkin' them to death."

"What are you talking about, Frank?"

"I think you know."

McGrath said, "Are you doing this because you miss your kids and you need to be a father to somebody?"

"Now don't get touchy on me, Colin. Maybe you're right about that, but that doesn't change the fact that you're making yourself miserable. You're still a young man and you have no folks. I'm three times your age and if I want to give you some fatherly advice, then you ought to be smart enough to listen."

McGrath lowered his head and said, "Alright, Frank, I'm listenin'."

"Ever work with sheep?" Jackson asked.

"I'm a cowman. What do you think?"

"Well I have," said Jackson. "Now, don't look at me like that. There's nothing wrong with a sheep. Where do you think wool comes from? And sometimes after a long winter, a good greasy mutton chop tastes as good as a beef steak. When I was a boy we ran a few sheep. You have to cut off their tails, you know. My grandfather showed me how to do that. You don't saw it off, you don't gnaw it off, you don't worry it off with a dull blade. And you don't try not to think about it and leave the job undone altogether. You do it slick and quick. Some things in life are like that. You decide what to do and then you do it."

When the knock came on the door, Ruth told herself it wasn't McGrath. She had been doing that for weeks: telling herself it wasn't him and trying to convince herself that she didn't care one way or the other.

Bonnie was holding Lyssa and she said, "Are you going to get that?"

Ruth set her features in a neutral expression and opened the door. "Colin," she said trying to keep her voice as neutral as her countenance, "Come in."

Lyssa jumped down from Bonnie's lap and rushed to McGrath. He bent and scooped her up and immediately began tickling her. Bonnie greeted him and he was invited into the kitchen for a bite to eat.

Lyssa sat on his lap while he ate and the talk flowed quite freely; they were all good friends. Presently Ruth took Lyssa away to put her to bed and McGrath said, "Bonnie, does Ruth ever . . ."

"Ever what?"

"Ever mention me?"

Bonnie laughed and McGrath reddened. She said, "Why, you fool, just ask her."

"But will she . . ."

Bonnie shook her head, "No Colin. I won't help you with this. This is something that isn't supposed to be easy. Just ask her."

Ruth came back in and sat down. Bonnie rose and started to leave the room and McGrath blurted out, "Ruth, will you marry me?"

Bonnie lost control completely, laughing so hard the tears flowed. Ruth watched her for a moment and then began to laugh too. And McGrath sat there looking miserable.

Each time it appeared that Bonnie was through laughing, she would suddenly start up again. Finally she left the room.

Ruth was finished laughing. Serious now, she said to him, "Shall we go for a walk?"

Outside in the darkness they strolled arm in arm and Ruth said, "In answer to your question, Colin, no."

"Sure," he muttered, "I understand."

Pulling her around, he started them back toward the house and said, "Well, I need to get going."

"Don't you even want to know why I've turned you down?"

"If a woman doesn't want to marry a man, I don't guess it really matters why."

"Of course it matters. What a stupid thing to say, Colin."

"I don't seem to be able to say anything right tonight," he said, sounding hurt.

"Apparently not," she agreed. She stopped and turned to face him. He turned to face her. She said, "There was a time when you did not consider me to be good enough for you because I had been willing to marry a man I didn't love just a week after my husband's death. Do you remember?"

"Of course I remember," said McGrath, "but . . ." He stopped, unable to think of anything more to say.

"I'm still that same woman. I haven't changed. And though I feel foolish for having offered to marry Frank, I don't know that I wouldn't do the same thing again if I found myself in those same circumstances. Do you understand what I'm saying, Colin?"

He dropped his eyes and nodded. They walked on back to the house. McGrath said goodbye to Bonnie from the doorway and turned to Ruth. "Well, so long."

"Goodbye, Colin." She went in and closed the door and he went to his horse.

He rode over to the saloon, went in, stopped halfway to the bar and turned around and walked back out. He rode down the street and took the trail to Double Circle. As he rode, his mind was flooded with memories and the whole long sequence of events, starting back home when his father and brother were still alive, passed through his consciousness. He had fought every battle with all the fight that was in him. He had not backed away from any of it, not from Mustin, not from Santry, not from Decker, not from anyone. He was not a man to back down or ride away from a problem.

But he was doing that now.

After McGrath left, Bonnie said to Ruth, "I'm so sorry, dear. You can go ahead and cry. It's alright."

"No," said Ruth.

They sat together in the kitchen and sipped tea, talking about many things, but avoiding the one subject Ruth did not want to discuss.

After a while, there was another knock on the door and Bonnie said, "I'll get it." She went to the door and Ruth heard her say, "Hello again, Colin. Come in."

His boots sounded on the floor, his spurs jingling with each step. He came into the kitchen and Bonnie invited him to sit.

"No thanks. I think I'll stand."

There was something different about him this time and Bonnie knew what it was. She left the room.

When they were alone, McGrath said to Ruth, "I'm sorry."

"For what?"

"For being a fool. You're a better woman than I'll ever deserve. And I mean that, Ruth."

"I forgive you."

"I love you," he said, "and I think you love me. Is there anything else we need to talk about?"

"Not a thing," she said, coming into his arms.

There were four of them. They referred to themselves as 'The Delegation' and they were having a wonderful time on the train, chatting with each other, joking, watching the countryside slip by. But when it came time to get off they were ready.

Mandy Jackson, Frank's oldest child, the organizer of the trip and self-appointed leader of The Delegation was the first one off the train. Tom, tall and lean, Frank's youngest child and the only one who was not married, was complaining that he was hungry.

"I'm sure there'll be someplace to eat," said Mandy, and with the men carrying the luggage, they all walked up the street.

"There's a hotel right over there," said Stan.

"That's where we're going," said Mandy. "What did you think?"

They took two rooms in the hotel and left their luggage and went outside to have a look around.

Tom said, "I'm still hungry."

"There's a restaurant just down the street," said Carol.

It was Bonnie's restaurant. They walked in and sat down and Stan said, "Order for me would you? I'm going to go make some inquiries."

"Good," said Mandy, "we'll do the same here."

An attractive young blonde woman came to take their order. Tom flirted a little with her and Mandy kicked him under the table.

They ordered their food and when it was brought to them Mandy asked the blonde waitress if she knew of a Frank Jackson.

Ruth smiled and said, "Why yes, I do."

Just then Stan came in and interrupted. He acted excited. Ruth left to take care of some other customers, but her curiosity had been aroused and as she moved around the room, she made an effort to listen to the conversation. Frank Jackson had told her about his children and she was sure these were some of them.

Carol said, "Stan you smell of liquor."

"I went to a saloon to get information. I had a drink. That's what you do in a saloon. Anyway, here's the story. Father bought a ranch near here and somehow got involved in a range war. And get this— he won. Then the territorial governor himself came to town, just to help Father. He told everyone that Father was his good friend and had saved his life during the war in Mexico. After he left, the main instigator of the range war, some guy named Treadwell, was mighty unhappy about the whole thing. He and Father had a gunfight right out there on the street and Father shot him."

"Shot him?" said Carol. "Killed him?"

"No. He's not dead, but he killed the town marshal, so they're probably going to hang him. He was a pretty bad man. He kept his wife locked up for eight years. He paid some woman to keep watch on her. They put that woman in jail too. But there's more, a whole lot more. Something about Father being trapped in a mine for about a week, and did you know he hangs around with some gunfighter named McGrew or McGraw?" Stan stopped and licked his lips, grinning. "But the best part . . . you'll never guess the best part."

"What?" said Carol, breathlessly.

Stan sat there, smiling maliciously, not speaking.

"Tell us!" demanded Mandy.

"He's engaged to some woman. Our Father is getting married."

Tom and Stan looked at each other and exchanged a leering grin. Mandy and Carol were shocked. Carol said she refused to believe it, and Mandy said, "I only hope he was smart enough not to get involved with some gold digger."

"Or some old hag," said Tom.

Up to now Ruth had been struggling to keep from laughing out loud, but this angered her a little. She went into the kitchen and conferred with Bonnie.

Bonnie came out, speaking affably to the patrons. Everyone seemed to know her, everyone seemed to like her. She came over to the table where The Delegation sat. "How is your food?"

"Actually we haven't started it yet," said Mandy. "But it looks very good."

"Are you new in town or just passing through?"

"We won't be staying long," said Mandy.

"Well, I hope you enjoy your visit here, and you'd better eat that food before it cools off. If there's anything I can do for you, just let me know."

After Bonnie went back into the kitchen, Carol said, "I hope it's someone like her."

Mandy nodded her agreement.

Tom said, "She's too young, too pretty. Father's old."

Ruth came over, ostensibly to check on the group, and said, "Earlier you asked me if I knew Frank Jackson."

"Yes," said Mandy.

"It happens that I do. In fact I know him quite well. Before he got engaged to Bonnie—the woman you just met—I tried to get him to marry me." She allowed the silence to stretch out for a moment and then said, "But he turned me down." She smiled. "Enjoy your food, it's getting cold." She turned and walked back into the kitchen.

And for a while none of Frank Jackson's children said a word.

*

OFFICIAL WEBSITE
authorcmcurtis.com

FOLLOW C.M. ON FACEBOOK
facebook.com/authorcmcurtis

.

Made in the USA
Lexington, KY
09 November 2016